Christie &Company

Down East

Other Avon Books by
Katherine Hall Page

CHRISTIE & COMPANY

Christie &Company
Down East

KATHERINE HALL PAGE

AVON BOOKS  NEW YORK

This is a work of fiction. Names, characters, places, and incidents either are the product of the author's imagination or are used fictitiously. Any resemblance to actual events, locales, organizations, or persons, living or dead, is entirely coincidental and beyond the intent of either the author or the publisher.

AVON BOOKS
A division of
The Hearst Corporation
1350 Avenue of the Americas
New York, New York 10019

Copyright © 1997 by Katherine Hall Page
Map by Virginia Norey
Interior design by Kellan Peck
Visit our website at **http://AvonBooks.com**
ISBN: 0-380-97396-0

Library of Congress Cataloging in Publication Data:

Page, Katherine Hall.
  Christie & Company down east / Katherine Hall Page.
      p.   cm.
Summary: Friends and mystery lovers Christie, Maggie, and Victoria try to discover who is sabotaging the inn run by Maggie's parents.
[1. Hotels, motels, etc.—Fiction. 2. Mystery and detective stories.] I. Title.
PZ7.P142Chi 1997   96-31431
[Fic]—dc20   CIP

First Avon Books Printing: April 1997

AVON TRADEMARK REG. U.S. PAT. OFF. AND IN OTHER COUNTRIES, MARCA REGISTRADA, HECHO EN U.S.A.

Printed in the U.S.A.

FIRST EDITION

OPM   10 9 8 7 6 5 4 3 2 1

❖❖❖

For Amy Lauren Fine—
a member of our "Company"

Acknowledgments

The author would like to thank her agent, Faith Hamlin, and her editor, Gwen Montgomery, for their help—and friendship.

"This affair must all be unraveled from within."

—Agatha Christie,
The Mysterious Affair at Styles

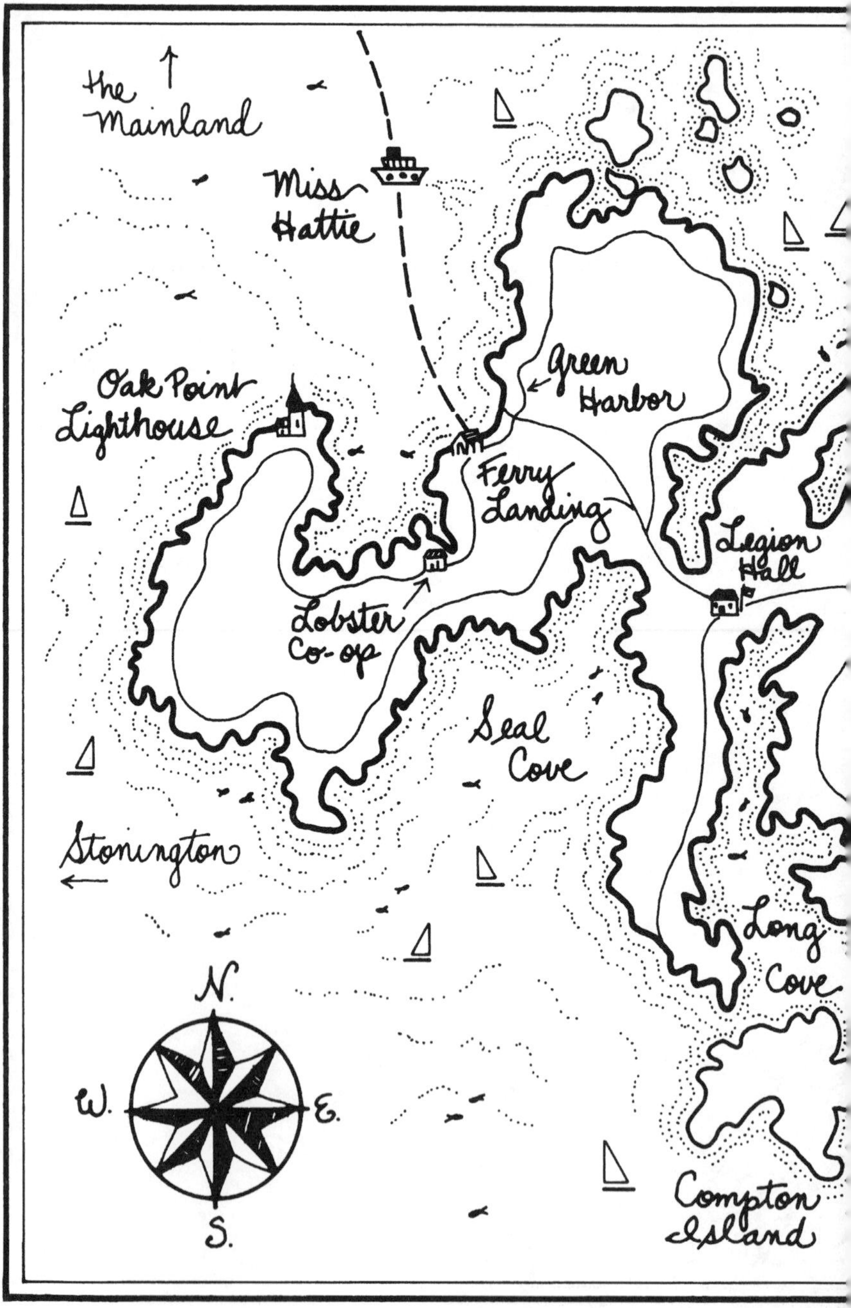
the Mainland
Miss Hattie
Oak Point Lighthouse
Green Harbor
Ferry Landing
Legion Hall
Lobster Co-op
Seal Cove
Stonington
Long Cove
N.
W.
E.
S.
Compton Island

the Blue Heron Inn

↑ Mount
Desert
Island

Caroline Griffith's
House

Sanford
Cove

Old
Granite
Quarry

the
Lily Pond

Proposed Site for
"Isle Away"

Potato
Island

Little Bittern Island,
Maine

❖Chapter One

THE TROUBLES AT THE BLUE HERON INN started when Maggie Porter's friends from school arrived.

Maggie was sitting cross-legged on the Little Bittern landing, watching the gradual transformation of the ferry, *Miss Hattie,* from a tiny black dot on the horizon to a seaworthy vessel somewhat in need of paint. Maggie drummed her fingers impatiently on the rough planks of the wharf. The boat seemed to be taking forever!

The sun was setting over Maine's Penobscot Bay. Glorious purple, orange, and rose streaks colored the clouds, creating strange configurations in the waning light. But Maggie barely noticed the sight stretched out in front of her. She was mad. This whole day— a day that was supposed to have been one filled with happy anticipation—had been ruined. By Mom. As usual.

All along, Maggie had assumed she'd take the ferry over and be on the mainland to greet her friends Christie Montgomery and Vicky Lee, then ride back with them. But when she'd mentioned it to her

1

mother that morning, Mrs. Porter had been firm. It was a waste of money, and besides, she needed her daughter at the inn.

Maggie had blown up: "Since when is spending money on friendship a 'waste'! Some welcome— they're not even going to know where they are, and they'll be tired after the bus trip from Boston. I just hope they'll make the right changes in Portland and Ellsworth. They *need* me to be there!" Her mother had seemed amused, which only increased Maggie's fury.

"I'm sure they can find their way. They're big girls, and once you're on the dock, the only place to go *is* the island, so don't worry about your friends. They'll be here before you know it," she'd said. Maggie's ten-year-old brother, Willy, had picked that inauspicious moment to enter the inn's kitchen, where the drama was unfolding.

"What's Maggie on about this time?" he'd asked his mother.

"None of your business, you little creep!" Maggie shouted. He was constantly prying into her private life! Of course she got yelled at for calling her brother a name—a name that, Maggie argued, suited him perfectly.

Lately, all she had to do was be in the same room with her mother and sparks would fly. They'd always had their ups and downs, but in the last couple of years, the downs had outnumbered the ups. The two had been on the verge of a major battle ever since Maggie had returned home from school. Willy, of course, could do no wrong, and Maggie wasn't getting along with him, either. Slightly put out—after all, she had been gone the entire year, except for vacations—she'd turned to her father, who was the same as always: loving, understanding—and right in the middle.

And Mom, having said she needed Maggie, made sure her daughter didn't have an idle moment until it was time to meet the ferry. Maggie had been tempted to answer back when her mother told her she could go to the landing—"Thanks, your majesty," or maybe something a little more original—but she sped out the door instead. All she needed was to be grounded. "They'll be here before you know it." It was just the kind of thing parents always said—and it had been totally wrong.

The day had inched by so slowly that Maggie thought her watch must surely have broken, and she checked the tall grandfather clock in the living room constantly, only to find annoying agreement with her watch.

Now sitting on the dock, she had more time—time to think. At first, it had been great to be home after the busy school year, but something was in the wind, and it wasn't just her mother who was snappish and on edge. The guests at the inn seemed to be a more demanding, complaining bunch than usual, and Maggie watched her father's normally even temper get severely tested several times. But it was hard to describe what was wrong. It was kind of like having a tender spot in your mouth that could erupt into a full-blown canker sore at any moment. Or worse, a tiny red dot on your face that might mushroom into a zit overnight. Maggie wanted to be a writer. Metaphors and similes regularly marched through her thoughts. Well, whatever it was—or was like—she wished it would go away. Awakening each day with a slight feeling of uneasiness was beginning to get to her. If anything was going to change things, it would be the presence of her friends. No more creepy thoughts, she admonished herself. This was going to be a perfect visit. It was just her imagination, her "overactive imagination," according to Mom.

Nothing could possibly go wrong.

She stood up. The boat loomed larger and larger. She waved, but it was still too far away to tell which of the tiny ants on the upper deck were her friends. Watching the *Miss Hattie,* named for the island's postmistress, Maggie's mood changed abruptly. She stretched her arms out in excitement and ran to the end of the landing. They were almost here!

The three girls had met the previous fall. The only new eighth graders at The Cabot School in Aleford, Massachusetts, they had been roommates and then quickly became close friends—a tie that grew even stronger when they solved a mystery plaguing the school. It was during this time that the girls, all avid whodunit readers, dubbed themselves "Christie & Company." After all, hadn't Christie been named for Agatha Christie? Her parents had picked the name to commemorate the way they'd met: sitting across from each other on the subway, each reading Christie's *Death on the Nile.*

But Molly Montgomery's life had been cut short.

She died of breast cancer the spring before Christie entered Cabot. Christie's father, Calvin Montgomery, a lawyer, traveled a great deal, and he worried that his daughter would be lonely, even with a housekeeper, in their town house on Boston's Beacon Hill. Cabot, located west of the city, seemed a good choice.

The third member of Christie & Company, Victoria Lee, had been born in Hong Kong, shortly before her parents came to the United States. "I'll never be able to be President," she'd complained to her friends. "Does the Vice President have to be born here, too?" Vicky's parents owned a popular Cantonese restaurant, the Ginger Jar, in Brookline, Massachusetts, just outside Boston. It kept them busy seven days a week, and they began to worry about Vicky. Vicky didn't see why she couldn't look after herself, and her elderly grandmother *did* live with them, so it wasn't as if she was completely on her own. But her parents were insistent, and so Vicky found herself, as she told her Brookline friends, "in the boonies, where the only eligible male on campus is the kid from Aleford who has the school as part of his paper route." Fortunately, Mansfield Hill Academy, a school for boys, was in Aleford, too.

Maggie had arrived at Cabot, her mother's old school, after a year of commuting by ferry to school on the mainland. The island of Little Bittern had only an elementary school, and Maggie's daily trip had been exhausting and occasionally impossible. Several times during the winter, bad weather had prevented the crossing and she'd had to stay with friends of the family—once for a whole week. Some students moved to the mainland during these months and boarded. Maggie certainly hadn't been seeing that much of her family, and as a devoted alum, Julia Porter had always wanted her daughter to follow in her footsteps. With great trepidation, Maggie had left for Cabot on an alumnae scholarship. What would the girls be like? she'd wondered. And it was a long way from home—plus, following in Mom's footsteps was an activity Maggie had been increasingly avoiding.

She could see her friends now and began waving wildly and shouting. They called back, but it was impossible to make out the words over the boat's engine and the raucous cries of the gulls circling overhead. Then, with a rattling shudder and a long moan, *Miss Hattie* came to a grinding halt.

"Maggie! Maggie!" Vicky and Christie shouted in unison. They were waiting with the rest of the passengers for the cars to be unloaded first.

"I can't believe you're really here!" Maggie called back.

"Exactly where are we, by the way?" Vicky asked. "You said the island was remote, but I feel like I've been traveling for days!" Christie laughed and nodded in agreement. Crossing over to the island at the point where water and sky were all she'd been able to see, she'd felt as if she was at the edge of the world.

"Don't worry," Maggie assured them, "you haven't crossed any time zones."

She hadn't seen her roommates for almost three whole weeks, and it felt longer. But of course nothing had changed. Vicky managed to appear as if she had just showered and put on fresh clothes. Her long, thick, straight dark hair was pulled back in a low ponytail. She wore a short bright blue slip dress over a hot-pink T-shirt. Silver bangles, probably from her favorite bargain haunt, Filene's Basement in downtown Boston, covered one wrist. Her oversized sunglasses were perched on her head. Christie looked as unrumpled, but her clothes were all standard Gap and her sleek blond hair, kept short for her diving, never looked messy. Maggie knew what she'd look like if their places were switched: as if she'd spent all day on the bus. At Vicky's suggestion, she was letting her reddish brown hair grow again. Last winter, she'd ill-advisedly had it cut short and ended up with a mess of unruly curls. It was getting better, but she still avoided mirrors. Unsure about her appearance for as long as she could remember, she'd never been a looking-glass fan—unlike Vicky, who constantly checked herself out in any surface that reflected.

"We'll be right there!" Christie called as she and Vicky disappeared to gather up their bags.

While Maggie waited, she thought about how important her friends were to her, especially during those first days at Cabot. She remembered what she'd felt as this same boat had docked last fall and she'd stepped on for the trip to the school: pure terror. The girls in the pictures in the school catalog had all looked like Miss Perfects. Maggie automatically stuck her hands in her jeans pockets. She had graduated from nail biter to sometime nail picker with the help of her friends. Maggie had lived in New

York City until she was nine and her parents bought the inn, but when she'd walked through the door of the eighth-grade dorm, Prentiss House, that September night, she'd felt like a total bumpkin. It had taken awhile for her to realize that even the girls who intimidated her most were not as sophisticated as they seemed. It was nice to think that next fall she wouldn't have to go through all that again. She sighed.

"Are you daydreaming again?" It was Vicky—and she was at Maggie's side. Christie stood behind her, grinning. Maggie had a pronounced tendency to go off to another world, and it was sometimes hard to get through.

Maggie grabbed them both in a big hug.

"No. Just thinking how lucky I am to have you for friends. Now let's find Darnell and the car. I can't wait to show you the Blue Heron."

"Who's Darnell?" Christie asked.

"Darnell Sanford. He's an islander. He takes care of the grounds and helps Dad with the boats. He went off to do an errand, but he must be back by now."

He wasn't, so the girls sat down on a huge log, washed up by a winter storm, at the top of the rocky shore to wait for him. The dark pink wild *Rosa rugosa* bushes that grew profusely above the high-water mark were still visible in the twilight. Christie took a deep breath of the cool, sharp air mixed with the strong fragrance of the roses. The colors of the setting sun had muted, leaving an orange glow. Against this backdrop, the jagged rows of pines to the rear of the landing looked as if someone with skill and sharp scissors had cut a frieze from black paper. The evening star was out. Christie made a wish. It was going to be a great month.

All the passengers had disembarked, heading for the small parking lot, waiting friends, and relatives. All save one—a woman. Christie had noticed her on the trip over. She had stood outside, in the bow of the ferry, even when the wind had whipped up the waves, creating a fine salt spray that forced everyone else indoors.

Now she seemed to be searching the parking lot for someone. She was walking about and glancing into the cars and pickup trucks that were departing quickly. Suppers on the table. Jobs to be done. Vacations beginning. The woman's face looked anxious as she watched until the lot was empty. No, Christie corrected herself. Not just anxious. Frightened. She nudged Maggie and, lowering her voice, asked, "Do you know who that is?" Maggie stood up and looked.

Tall and slender, the woman was about her parents' age, Maggie thought. She was dressed simply in well-worn jeans and an oversized gray sweatshirt. There was nothing particularly distinctive about her except for her hair. She'd tied it back with a scarf and it tumbled down her back in long waves—red, or to be more precise, Maggie observed—auburn waves. It reminded her of a picture she'd seen in one of her mother's art books. The woman in the painting had the same color hair and carried a rose; she was dressed like someone from Shakespeare. Her mother said it was the work of a Pre-Raphaelite artist, Dante

Gabriel Rossetti, an Englishman. Whoever this mystery woman was, her hair was straight out of that painting. Yet it didn't match her age. The hair was young, but her face looked much older.

"No, I've never seen her before," Maggie answered, then sat down again on the log. Darnell still wasn't there. "And I would certainly remember. She's not coming to the inn. Or at least she's not expected, and with July Fourth coming up, we're full! Sometimes people just show up, and it's a big pain. She must be coming to visit someone, though—someone who's late."

"What incredible hair," Vicky said. "I wonder how she keeps it so shiny?"

"Maybe we'll run into her again and the two of you can exchange beauty secrets," Christie teased. She did hope they would encounter the woman again, though. She wanted to know who she was and what the look on her face meant.

"Isn't the sunset wonderful!" Maggie exclaimed, her long, angry day totally forgotten. "I knew it would be, but it's been a little foggy lately, so I wasn't sure." Maggie wanted everything to be at its best while they were on the island. For a fleeting moment, she understood how parents felt when their kids misbehaved in public.

"Mags, slow down," Vicky reassured her. "We don't care. We're here—that's enough. And in my case, it's a miracle. I can't believe my parents agreed to let me come! Whatever your mother said should be bottled. They would almost never let me go on sleepovers when I was little, let alone spend a month at an inn on an island with no way off except this." Vicky waved her hand at *Miss Hattie* with its well-worn planks.

"My Dad wasn't too sure, either," Christie said. "It wasn't anything about safety. He thought I might get in the way and that there wouldn't be enough for me to do—that I'd be bored! And he was worried I'd miss my diving." Christie had been concerned about not diving for a month, too. She couldn't let herself get rusty—not after the great year she'd had. But it was an island, surrounded, of course, by water, so at least she could keep in shape by swimming, and maybe she could find a safe rock from which to dive.

"Not enough to do! I'm only afraid Mrs. Simon Legree, also known as Mom, will work us to death," Maggie complained. Surprisingly, the idea of inviting her daughter's roommates to the inn had been Mrs. Porter's. She'd written to Maggie about the possibility in May. "You may find life on the island a little lonesome after your lively year. Why not invite Christie and Vicky to come for a month?" At first, Maggie hadn't been sure about the plan. She'd resented her mother's implication that she might have changed, "outgrown" the island she loved so much. She didn't have to import entertainment. Besides, she had plenty of friends on Little Bittern from elementary school and her one year spent commuting. Charlene Compton was her best friend, and they had written to each other constantly.

But Charlene would be working at the lobster Co-Op this summer, and the rest of the kids would have jobs, too. There usually weren't that many families at the inn, or if there were, the children tended to be younger. And a little of Willy went a long way. He'd been seriously into puns and practical jokes during Maggie's spring vacation—a ten-year-old's versions. Much as Maggie hated to admit it, her mother had come up with a good idea.

After many letters and phone calls, everything was set. Christie and Vicky would join the staff at the Blue Heron. In exchange for room, board, and pocket money, they'd help the housekeeper and wait on tables. The inn served breakfast and dinner. Guests either took a box lunch or foraged for themselves in Green Harbor, the only real town on the island. Little Bittern's population doubled in the summer, but there weren't any traffic jams. It was expensive to bring a car over, and guests at the inn were encouraged to leave theirs on the mainland. The Blue Heron provided outings, on land and sea—and plenty of bicycles.

"Are there a lot of guests?" Vicky was intrigued by the idea of working at an inn. She'd done almost every job except cook at the Ginger Jar, yet this would be very different. For one thing, people didn't get up and go home after the meal.

"The season doesn't really start until the Fourth of July, but there are always some people who like to come early. Oh! I almost forgot. We've been pretty excited. Sybil Corcoran, who writes for *Gracious Living Magazine,* is doing a feature on us. Mom is a nervous wreck. She's outdoing herself at dinner and everything's going fine."

"*Gracious Living*—that would be tremendous publicity. No wonder your mother's nervous. I hope I don't drop dinner in the woman's lap or something," Christie said.

"What's she like?" Vicky asked. "Sophisticated and glamorous, right? With a knack for making potpourri from dandelions or turning bits of driftwood into ravishing picture frames." She spoke the last words in a snooty, through-the-nose tone of voice.

"I don't know about the picture frames and the dandelions—we have daisies now, anyway—but she does talk like that a bit and her nail polish matches her toes, which I'm sure you'll appreciate, Vic. She wears really stylish clothes and these big straw hats with scarves tied around them. The Maine coast is 'quite provincial' compared with the Hamptons—I heard her tell one of the guests that. She also mentioned that it's where she'd normally be this time of year—like we're so uncool. I keep wanting to tell her all these outrageous things—that there are a population of giant rabbits on the island or her toilet is broken and she'll have to use the privy, but of course I wouldn't! So far, I think she likes us—she's scarfing everything down at dinner and making a million notes in this little black leather notebook she carries around. 'My life, my entire life,' she calls it."

"Who else?" Christie was looking forward to checking out the inn's inhabitants. Maggie was the one who wanted to be a professional writer, but all three considered themselves keen observers of human nature, as detectives have to be.

"Sybil's nephew, Paul, is with her. When Mom told me he was coming, I thought he was going to be a whole lot more interesting. He's twenty-nine, lives in New York City, and is working on a novel. Dad's letting him use a small cabin out in the woods for his writing, and he goes there after breakfast every day, takes his lunch, and doesn't come out until dinner. Willy and I have gone to spy on him a couple of times, but all we heard was typing—he has this big old manual typewriter that belongs in some museum—and once he swore. There's no electricity or water out there. He has a camping lantern for dark days, and he really *does* have to use the outhouse."

The girls giggled.

"Has he ever published anything?" Vicky asked.

"Not that I know of. I'd love to talk to him about being a writer, except so far, he hasn't seemed exactly approachable."

Vicky got right to the point. "You haven't told us the most important thing—is he cute?"

"Sorry, not even *I* can work up a crush on him." Maggie was very susceptible to most guys' charms. "Not gross, just nothing special. Maybe his face changes when he smiles and he gets that special light in his eyes when the right person walks into the room, but I haven't seen it."

"Oh, Maggie, I've missed that imagination—and mouth—of yours!" Christie exclaimed. "Now, tell us about the others."

"A lot of couples who've just dropped a kid off at camp, or at least that's what I've imagined. The man looks happy and relaxed; the woman looks guilty and relaxed. You know, like she's really happy to be on vacation without little screaming whoever, but mean-

14

while she's picturing him falling off a horse or turning over in his canoe."

"No kids at all?" Vicky was asking because one of their jobs was to oversee the children's dinnertime, separate and earlier than the parents', plus provide some sort of entertainment afterward. With this in mind, she'd read some books on how to give children's birthday parties, and she didn't want the time she'd spent relearning SPUD and Duck, Duck, Goose to go to waste.

"None so far, but don't worry, there'll be plenty. The only offspring are the St. Clairs, and they're not arriving until tomorrow, although her parents are here."

"I missed a chapter," Christie said. "St. Clairs, plural, but only her parents? And where are the little darlings?"

" 'Little darlings' is right, or, to be precise, little darling. Roberta, named after her father, Robert—and remind me not to do that to any child of mine—is twenty-three, and a blushing new bride. I've watched her not grow up for years. You won't believe what a spoiled brat she is. Even Willy is more mature. She and her parents, Lucinda and Robert Bishop, lived in our building in New York. The Bishops were my parents' not-so-silent partners when they bought the inn. To make a long story short—and it's a very boring one—Aunt Lucinda and Uncle Bob—we're supposed to call them that—have been paid back, but they've been coming for a free vacation every summer, since my parents are so grateful to them, and of course 'little' Roberta has, too. I thought this year we'd be spared the company of 'Bobbie,' but she's coming straight here from her honeymoon with her new hubby, sailing their very own boat up from Newport. She is to gag. To give you an idea, the boat is named *Liquid Assets*."

"But shouldn't they all be paying guests now that the debt has been repaid? How do your parents feel about them?" asked practical Vicky. From the Ginger Jar, she knew how little it could take to turn the black ink to red. You wanted to keep as wide a profit margin as possible. She imagined a seasonal business would be even worse.

"You know what parents are like when it comes to judging people. Dense. They're so grateful the Bishops loaned them the money in the first place that they'd never ask them to pay to stay here. They actually seem to like them, although last summer Mom did get a little huffy about the way Bobbie was ordering Malvina around, asking her to wash her unmentionables, that kind of thing."

"Who's Malvina? I've never heard that name." Bored on this island, impossible! Christie thought to herself. It was fun sitting on the log, watching the sun go down, and hearing all about the inn. She didn't care how long it took Darnell to finish whatever he had to do.

"Malvina Compton, my friend Charlene's grandmother, is the housekeeper. You'll get to know her really well. She has a great sense of humor, but she doesn't put up with any nonsense. There are also a couple of women from the island working part-time with her and in the kitchen. It's always been hard for us to get help, and I'm not sure why. Maybe we can solve that mystery." Maggie smiled. "My parents pay well and there aren't a whole lot of jobs on Little Bittern, so it is kind of strange. But we've been lucky to have Malvina. She's been with the inn since the first season. My mom says anyone who could make it through that summer could make it through anything."

"What happened?" Vicky and Christie said together. Then they linked their pinkies and said, "Jinx" for luck.

"Some weeks, we had nobody; others, we were overbooked. Mom was preparing way too elaborate meals and never got out of the kitchen. The boat went aground and Dad and the guests had to wait for the next tide, which meant being on the boat overnight. Willy got chicken pox and gave it to a man who'd never had it. It's a lot worse for adults, and the man ended up in Blue Hill Hospital. And this is only the half of it!"

A blue minivan with the name of the inn on the side swung into the parking lot. Maggie jumped up and waved to the driver. "Come on. It's Darnell. Let's go."

Settled in the car with all their belongings, the girls started chatting again. Suddenly, Christie said, "Look, there's that woman—the one from the ferry." She was walking along the side of the road. "I wonder where she's going?"

Maggie leaned over the front seat. "Do you know who that is?" she asked Darnell. He glanced out the window. "Nope, can't say that I do." Then he paused and the car swerved ever so slightly. "But that hair . . ." He seemed to be talking to himself. Maggie had leaned back and was chatting to her friends again. She didn't hear his last muttered remark, but Christie caught it: "If it is her, there'll be trouble for sure."

A few minutes later, he called over his shoulder, "Hope you ladies don't mind if I just dump you and your tackle on the front porch. George's engine is acting up."

"Is George the name of his boat, or another car?" Christie asked Maggie.

"Neither. George is his son—and he lobsters. He's got his own boat. George works at the inn sometimes with Darnell," she added.

"Hmmmm," Vicky commented. "How old is he?"

"He's sixteen," Maggie answered, blushing deeply. Her roommates looked at each other.

"Oh, Maggie!"

❖ Chapter Two

MAGGIE OPENED HER EYES, SAT UP, AND stretched. She'd been dreaming, but she was having trouble remembering what it had been about. Not a good dream, though. She felt uneasy. Someone was running, and then she'd awakened. Who was it? Running away from something or someone. The more she tried to bring them back, the fainter the dream images became.

She looked about the room where they were sleeping. Her parents were gradually renovating all the guest cottages and had turned one over to the girls not yet begun. The inn itself was an enormous late-nineteenth-century "cottage" built by a wealthy New York businessman for his family's summer vacations. These summer people were known as "rusticators." They delighted in early-morning dips in the chilly waters, long walks through the woods, and, of course, sailing. Maggie had seen pictures of the inn taken at the time, with the family arranged on the front porch steps. She'd made up stories about them, especially about one little girl with long hair and an enormous bow sitting on top of her head. She wore a middy blouse and boy's knickers—pretty daring for that day.

Then, as now, the inn seemed as much a part of the coastal shoreline as the pines and granite rocks that stretched out on either side. The main house was perched high on a point—you could see the water from three sides—and it was a landmark for those at sea. A steep path led to the beach. A more gentle, sloping one went through the woods. The Porters had worked hard to make this path handicapped-accessible, and the first guest house they'd done over was also designed with that in mind.

Each generation of those original owners had added something—a boathouse, another cabin, storage sheds, even a gazebo. Mrs. Porter had planted her garden around the gazebo, mixing flowers and vegetables in carefully planned disarray. It was a favorite spot for afternoon tea or cocktails before dinner. When the Porters bought the inn, the estate had been abandoned for years and they purchased it from some kind of trust.

The cottage the girls were in consisted of two large rooms and a tiny bath with a shower that turned icy cold after three minutes. Maggie knew this was going to be a challenge for Vicky. She looked over at the other cots. Vicky! Her bed was empty! Up already? Christie was still sound asleep. They'd gone to bed early, after consuming big bowls of fragrant scallop stew, followed by strawberry shortcake, but then they'd talked late. Maggie grabbed her clothes and tiptoed out into the other room. It was flooded with sunshine from a large bay window facing the ocean.

The Porters had been using the cabin to store furniture in need of repair and surplus items. Last night, Maggie had apologized to the others for the odd assortment of chairs minus cane seats and the wobbly tables. Christie said it suited the place. Stacked against the pine walls were all sorts of framed pictures. They'd gone through one pile—faded watercolors, seascapes, some dark prints in fancy gilt frames of famous-looking paintings, and quite a few old photographs.

Maggie looked at her watch. Seven o'clock! One of her jobs was helping with breakfast, and she was going to be late. Her mother had said she could have the rest of the day off until dinner preparations to show Christie and Vicky around. Now, Mom would be so steamed at her, she'd probably make her scrub toilet bowls instead.

Maggie brushed her teeth furiously, yanked a comb through her hair, and sped out of the cabin. The inn wasn't far away, but you couldn't see it from the guest house. She sped up the path nearly knocking down Paul Corcoran, Sybil's nephew, the would-be author. She stopped short and for a moment they were eyeball-to-eyeball.

"Sorry," she stammered.

He seemed as embarrassed as she was. "No, my fault. I should be more careful. That's the thing, taking care, looking around you, noticing."

Maggie wondered if this was a line from whatever he was writing. If so, he was in trouble. In any case, it sounded weird.

"Well, I have to get going. I'm supposed to help with breakfast."

"Breakfast. Food, the staff of life . . ."

She was forced to leave him midsentence, running again when she was sure no one would be around the bend. She gave a passing thought to the state of his rumpled shirt and baggy jeans. He needed someone to take him in hand. She was surprised his aunt, the glamorous magazine writer, hadn't done so. He seemed eager to please her in every other way, attentively pulling out her chair at the table, running to fetch articles she needed from her room. She seemed to regard him as her personal servant. The only time Maggie had heard her say anything to him that wasn't an order was to compare him to his father—and it wasn't favorable. Maggie raced up the last part of the path and shot through the back door, straight into the kitchen. Paul Corcoran was immediately forgotten.

"I'm really, really sorry, Mom . . ." she began, and then paused. Vicky was standing at the counter stirring a large bowl of batter. She and Mrs. Porter had been chatting away like old friends. What is wrong with this picture? Maggie thought.

"Good morning, sleepyhead," Her mother said, but her voice was affectionate and amused, not scolding.

"You know what an early bird I am," Vicky said, winking at Maggie. "I came up here, and your mother let me take a shower in the family's bathroom. I didn't want to disturb you and Christie."

So that was it! Maggie should have figured it out. Sherlock, even Dr. Watson, would have. There was no way Victoria Lee was going to risk taking a cold shower.

"Your mother's been telling me how you came to have the inn and all the stuff she did beforehand. I had no idea it was so complicated. But it also sounds like fun." Vicky's eyes were shining. Another idea for her crowded future.

Maggie had heard the story many times—had lived through it—and it was true that her parents, particularly her mother, had worked as hard to prepare to buy an inn as they now did owning one. Julia Porter had enrolled in a course at the New School called Before You Start That Business, and every weekend the family left Manhattan to visit inns and eventually to check out places for sale. The Porters had all agreed on Maine, which focused their search. Ned Porter's grandparents had had a summer place on the coast and he'd always dreamed of living there. That farmhouse had passed out of the family's hands long before Maggie was born, but they'd taken vacations nearby. Ned was an expert sailor and thought he could add to the inn's appeal by offering day trips and sailing lessons. So they had to be on deep water. He'd also envisioned guests arriving in their own boats, which had indeed happened. Julia had been working in a carryout gourmet shop and she'd been a culinary arts major. She was counting on the inn's food to attract people, as well. They planned to open the dining room to the general public for dinner and Sunday brunch. She had dreams of a line of Blue Heron products—jams, chutneys. For Christmas the first year, Maggie had elaborately labeled an empty tin BLUE HERON AIR™ and wrapped it up for her mother, who now kept it displayed on one of the kitchen counters.

The Porters had wanted a slightly more accessible location, yet they had fallen in love with the house and the view—something the how-to books warned against. Over the next year as they struggled to get the inn open in time for the first guests, "Maybe we're crazy, but . . ." entered the family's lexicon as one long word.

The naming of the inn had been no problem. That first afternoon, a pair of great blue heron had flown directly overhead, slowly, elegantly. An omen, a good one. The herons continued to fly near the inn and the Porters' luck was holding. True, Ned still worked as a textbook editor and freelance writer—technology had enabled him to keep his jobs, even long distance. But he hoped to be able to give them up in a few years.

"Vicky's going to teach me some of her family's Cantonese specialties. It will be fun to have new things to add to the menus," Mrs. Porter said.

"If that chowder last night was anything to go by, I'd leave the menus alone," Christie said, coming in the door. Her hair was damp. She rarely bothered to dry it, and Maggie envied the way it always behaved, unlike her own unruly mop of curls. "But I love all the food at the Ginger Jar," she added. "Now, what's the drill? Do we eat first, then work, or the other way around?"

"It depends on when you get up." Mrs. Porter did send a look her daughter's way now—a look Maggie called "the evil eye." "We set the tables the night before, and officially breakfast starts at eight, but there are always some early risers who want to be off sailing or have planned some other outing. The first thing we do is put out a buffet of cold cereals, fruit, and some sort of muffin or scone, then start the coffee. Vicky and I have already done it."

Maggie was feeling rather dispensable—something that would have thrilled her ordinarily. She wondered why it bothered her now.

"We don't know how we're going to feed all these people, and more refugees are arriving by the hour. The UN airdrop has disappeared in the jungle. It's missed us by miles! What are we going to do?" Her assistant was close to hysteria. Dr. Porter pushed a strand of hair back from her wet brow. A specialist in alternative food sources, it was all up to her. She scanned the vegetation that closed in on them like a damp sponge. Her eyes lit upon one leaf in particular. Of course, Spiraea fernidoptera. *It was growing in abundance and it was indeed like a sponge, retaining water in its fleshy interior. They could chew the leaves and stems, warding off starvation for several days if necessary. "The world will soon know what you have done, Dr. Porter." Terence Cholmondeley, the head of the relief expedition, spoke the words low into her ear, following them with a soft—*

"Maggie! Are you woolgathering again!" Her mother's annoyed voice sliced through the air. "She does this sometimes," Mrs. Porter explained to her daughter's friends.

"We know," Christie said. "Earth to Maggie: Prepare to take orders. They can choose pecan waffles, eggs, oatmeal, and bacon. No sausage today, if anyone asks."

Mrs. Porter was handing out aprons, periwinkle blue ones with the name of the inn and a heron stenciled across the front. The colors and the motif appeared throughout the inn, from the stationery left in each room to the color of the shutters at the windows. At dinner, the wait staff wore white blouses and black pants or skirts, and there were tablecloths instead of place mats. Breakfast was more casual. The girls would be the only ones waiting on the guests. At night, they'd be filling in if one of the regulars couldn't make it. Christie looked at the back of Maggie's T-shirt and whispered, "Maybe you should turn your shirt around."

All the girls were mystery fans and great readers, but Maggie was the most serious. She had a collection of mystery T-shirts from various specialty bookshops around the country. Everyone knew what to get her for a present. Today's had the name of the store printed discreetly over the pocket and a fancy dagger lying in a pool of blood—full color—on the back.

"Thanks. No need to gross out the guests," she whispered back as she turned the shirt around where it would be hidden by the apron's bib.

She grabbed a pad and pencil, hurriedly pushing the "in" door, instead of the "out." "I know, I know," she said to her mother over her shoulder. Nothing was going right today.

She got busy taking orders. Everybody, it seemed, wanted the waffles. They would have been her choice, too—with lots of blueberry syrup.

It was hard to imagine that one family, albeit a large one, had occupied the enormous gray-shingled house. The dining room was directly behind the living room; the two were adjoining and shared a high vaulted wooden ceiling. A fieldstone fireplace, as huge as one of those medieval ones where they roasted whole sheep, divided the rooms. Its chimney went straight up the middle and a wide balcony on the second floor encircled both rooms. The living room was filled with comfortable chairs facing the long windows, which, contrary to usual Victorian practice, let in light—and, of course, the view. Maggie liked to sit in a big chair up in the balcony above the front door and read a mystery. Many of the bedrooms were off the balcony, including the family's own. They vacated these during the summer months, moving to smaller ones in an addition that had been tacked on to the rear of the house in the twenties. Maggie didn't mind the seasonal migration, yet she was always glad to unpack her special things and reclaim her space. Willy out-and-out hated it, grumbling at having to put away all his toys and move to what he considered a much-inferior room.

"Eggs with your waffles?" Maggie asked the last guest.

"Why not? It's vacation. Two, over and out."

She wrote it down and hurried to the kitchen. She

went through the right door this time, then froze as a bloodcurdling scream filled the air, immediately followed by the sound of breaking glass. She dropped the pad and ran back. Her mother, close behind her, pushed her to one side.

It was Sybil Corcoran, and she was completely hysterical. Several guests and her nephew were at her side, trying to find out what had happened.

"She reached into her pocketbook. She was making a joke about all the vitamin pills she takes; then she let out that yell and heaved the bag across the room at the bookcase," one man observed.

Christie and Vicky had not been far behind Mrs. Porter.

"What a shame she had to throw it that way," Christie whispered. "A little to the left and she would only have hit the wall. It's going to be hard to replace that glass."

Maggie nodded. "It belonged to my grandmother, and Mom really loves it." The bookcase in question had glass doors encased in elaborately carved swirls of wood. The glass had had a slightly wavy surface; Maggie and Willy liked to make faces in it when they were younger. Nobody could make any faces in the shards lying strewn about the floor.

"Maggie, get a broom and dustpan, please." Her mother was leading Ms. Corcoran to the other room.

"A fit over vitamin pills? I don't get it," Vicky said as Maggie walked past her on the way to the kitchen. Maggie shrugged. "Maybe she just got up on the very, very wrong side of the bed this morning."

"Sssh," said Christie, and the three girls heard Sybil's voice rise in a combination of fury and fear.

"Now, Mrs. Porter, I know I'm in the country, but I do *not* expect to put my hand on a dead rodent when I reach into my bag—a bag that has been tightly closed all night! No, I don't need to sit down. I need to scrub my hand!"

"Yuck, a dead mouse in her pocketbook. I don't blame her!" Vicky said.

Maggie's mother's tone was lower and less distinct. She was trying to reassure the guest at her side and all the ones unabashedly eavesdropping from the next room. One man was laughing. "What a show. The woman must have jumped a mile, and the way she fired that purse, you'd think she was Nolan Ryan!" He stopped abruptly at a look from his wife.

Mrs. Porter and her charge were returning to the breakfast tables. Maggie ran for the broom and Vicky went to get fresh coffee for the columnist. Vicky had heard professional writers lived on the stuff, so Vicky figured she'd probably want some right now. Sybil Corcoran was as Maggie had described, only smaller than Vicky had pictured her. But definitely Calvin Klein, not L. L. Bean. She had short dark hair, with not even one gray strand. It was slicked straight back and tucked behind her ears. Today she was wearing enormous gold hoop earrings. They matched the bright brass buttons on her crisp navy blazer. She was wearing white pants and a striped top—obviously a nautical theme.

"We'll see to it that your purse is thoroughly cleaned," Mrs. Porter was murmuring placatingly.

Christie, standing by the bookcase, watched them enter the room and thought she could read Mrs. Porter's mind, thoughts betrayed by a deep line between her eyes. Of all the people staying at the inn, why, oh why, did the mouse have to choose to expire in the bag of the person writing an article that they hoped would send them more guests than they could handle!

"I promise you nothing like this will happen again," Julia Porter said firmly.

But she was wrong.

❖Chapter Three

BY TEN O'CLOCK, EVERYONE, INCLUDING THE girls, had been fed and the full-time crew under Malvina Compton had taken over. The dead mouse had been properly disposed of and Mrs. Porter was taking the columnist to visit a well-known potter who lived on the island. Little Bittern had long attracted artists of all kinds. The potter's work had often graced the rooms of the houses in *Gracious Living Magazine,* so Sybil was eager to work him into her story. Afterward, they were going to see a basket maker who specialized in the difficult craft of pine needle baskets. By lunchtime, Mrs. Porter told the girls, Ms. Corcoran would be treating the mousecapade as a joke. She hoped.

Christie & Company were sitting on the beach, deciding how to spend their time off.

"Let's take sandwiches and ride bikes into Green Harbor. We can go see Charlene at the Co-Op."

"What's that?" Vicky asked.

"It's how the lobstermen sell their catch. Some people sell to a dealer who provides them with bait and fuel for the boat. The Co-Op does the same thing, only it's run by the lobstermen themselves."

Going to Green Harbor seemed like a good plan, although Christie was reluctant to leave the beach. The water was sparkling, the color changing from dark blue to aquamarine as the clouds overhead drifted by. She longed to dive in. She'd promised the Porters not to swim alone, and they'd warned her that the water was cold. It was warmer at other spots on the island, tidal waters, not deep water like where the inn was. There was also a small freshwater lily pond where people swam. But Christie knew she wouldn't mind how cold the water was, and she loved to swim in salt water. You were so buoyant.

"Don't you guys want to take a quick dip first?" she suggested optimistically.

"Not first, and maybe never," Vicky answered quickly. "I want to check out the lily pond. It sounds a whole lot more inviting."

Maggie noticed the disappointment on Christie's face. "We'll come back in enough time to swim. I've gotten used to it over the years, and when Vicky sees how much fun we're having, she'll jump in, too."

They climbed up the sharp incline, Vicky solemnly swearing that the one finger she'd put into the water gently lapping the beach was now frostbitten and that they were insane. At the top of the path, Willy was waiting.

"Are you going to Green Harbor? If you are, can I come, too? Mom said I could."

Maggie's mood had improved, but it quickly changed. She didn't want to inflict her younger brother on her friends or on herself.

"No, you can't come."

"But I'm not allowed to go by myself!"

"Then you'll have to wait until you're older, like I did."

"You are so mean. I hate you and your stupid friends! Just you wait!"

Vicky and Christie had been silent during the squabble. After Willy stormed off, Vicky said, "Maybe we can take him another time. He doesn't seem so bad. You should meet some of my cousins."

"Really, Maggie, we don't care," Christie told her.

"But I do, and he's a pest. Come on, let's go."

Maggie was madder than ever at Willy for spoiling the start of Christie & Company's first outing on the island.

They took off on their bikes down the long dirt road, which was covered with a thick carpet of pine needles. It led away from the inn and out onto the macadam of the main road that circled the island. Maggie's spirits rose as she heard her friends exclaim over various things as they rode along.

"Look, a lighthouse! Does it still work?" Vicky asked.

"Yes, except it's automated now. No lighthouse keeper and family. Malvina has lots of stories about them, though. I can't imagine being on a tiny island for months at a time with only your family. If it had been mine, I'm sure we'd never have made it past the first week. We'd have been back on the mainland—or killed each other off."

"It would have been lonely, but it also sounds romantic." Vicky imagined herself keeping the light going in the teeth of a gale, while the rest of her family was ill or stranded someplace far below the towering light, unable to help her.

In her thoughts, Christie focused on the word *lonely*. It was a word that occurred to her often. The lighthouse families had had one another. Maybe they had gotten lonely for other people, but the kind of loneliness Christie felt after losing her mother threatened to swallow her up with a force equal to any nor'easter. She still thought of her mother's death each day. Sometimes it would be with her as she woke up, a sharp stab of reality. Sometimes it would come, as now, when a word like *lonely* triggered it. For a long time, she had resented the fact that her father was the one who was alive, a father who had been away a great deal. Not like Molly Montgomery, who was with her daughter constantly. Christie loved her father and knew he had to work, but it had become a kind of weight she carried around in addition to her grief—the guilt. Finally, at Cabot, she'd been able to tell someone and was getting counseling. And of course it had been Vicky and Maggie she told. She took a few deep breaths as the counselor had taught her to—it stopped the feeling that she was going to faint. She forced her thoughts to the present. They were crossing a small causeway and the tide was way out. Rocks draped with glistening seaweed were completely exposed. Sandpipers on stiltlike legs darted among them, oblivious of the clammers bent over at the backbreaking task of digging for the increasingly scarce bivalves. Three black cormorants with their long, thin shepherd's-crook necks sat immobile on the top of one rock. Gulls and terns wheeled gracefully overhead.

Slowly, Christie felt herself emerge from her depression and begin to notice the beauty that surrounded them. She made herself call out to Maggie. "It's wonderful here. I'm really glad I came."

Maggie flashed her a grin. It was going to be a great day after all.

The ride to Green Harbor, which was on the opposite end of the island from the inn, was a long one. In the car, coming from the ferry, it hadn't seemed so far. Before they got there, they stopped and ate their sandwiches at the top of an old granite quarry, now abandoned. They were so high, they could see straight out to the other islands in Penobscot Bay. The air was clear and the sea was filled with white sails.

"There were two quarries in operation on the island at one time, also a sawmill and a large boatyard. Now fishing is the main industry, and that's pretty chancy. The boats have to go farther and farther out for their catch. There are still plenty of lobsters, though not like the old days. Malvina says she and her brothers and sisters used to beg their mother not to give them lobster again," Maggie told them.

"Everybody here knows how to do all sorts of things," she continued. "It's hard to depend on the sea for a living. There are a lot of summer people, but it's too far for most tourists—although some people take the ferry just for the ride. When they get to Green Harbor, there isn't much. There aren't a lot of quaint shops, thank goodness, and the inn is the only place to stay—at the moment."

"What do you mean? And it sounds like you're not happy about it," Christie asked.

"An off-islander, a guy named—if you can believe it—Hap Hotchkiss, is trying to develop a big piece of land on the eastern side of the island into a kind of resort community. He wants to call it Isle-Away. Get it?"

"Why would that be bad?" Vicky asked. "It couldn't take away from the inn's business, could it? Different kinds of people, I'd imagine."

"It probably couldn't hurt us, yet it would change the character of the island and open it up for further developments like that. Pretty soon, we'd be just like Bar Harbor. My dad is one of the selectmen, and he's been opposing it on all sorts of grounds, especially the impact it would have on the island's ecostructure. He and some other people have formed the Island Trust to try to buy certain pieces of land or get people to leave it to the trust in their wills. The problem is a jerk like Hap—and what could that be short for?—seems to have plenty of money to throw around. And people here need it."

Vicky leaned back, lay down, and closed her eyes. She hadn't even been here twenty-four hours and already she was feeling protective of Little Bittern.

"Happy," she mumbled. "Or Hapgood. Maybe Haphazaard." She was getting drowsy. She smelled the balsam from the pines that grew up to the rocks. She rested her head on a soft cushion of moss.

They were on a granite ledge that sloped down to

another, then another, and so on—like steps for a giant descending straight into the water.

The next thing she knew, Maggie and Christie were shaking her. "If we want to get to town and back in time, we have to leave right away," Maggie said. "I know you're an early bird, and I guess they get tired," she teased.

"I was just resting my eyes. It's so peaceful here. Lead me to Green Harbor!" Vicky jumped up and they resumed their trip.

Fifteen minutes later, they came into the town, which consisted of a post office and a small number of stores, among them a market that also sold sandwiches and soft drinks, a marine-supply and hardware store, and something that, judging from the window, sold a little bit of everything. Vicky stopped her bike in front and read aloud from the list painted in white paint on the large plate-glass windows: "Welcome To Our Island! We Have Fishing Supplies, Household Items, Toys, Collectibles, Candy, Lamp Oil, Pet Food, Greeting Cards, and Hosiery."

"We'll stop on the way back. It *is* pretty amazing. My Mom found a pair of shoes from the forties there once. They never get rid of any of their inventory, and they change the list from time to time. We all look forward to what's next."

The Co-Op was past the town wharf and ferry landing. The good-sized harbor was filled with boats of all sizes and types. One in particular stood out: a thirty-foot Tartan, its fresh white sails catching the wind as it left.

"Uh-oh," Maggie said. "I think we may be the first

lucky people to have glimpsed the St. Clair nuptial barge. They must have needed fuel." She pointed out the name on the stern, *Liquid Assets*. Some of the islanders were noting it, too. Maggie was sure it would be a topic of conversation the full length of the island and then some.

"Let's get going. At least we're prepared to see them later."

The girls followed her down the road, a steep hill that ended at another pier, with a low wooden building—a fish cannery now closed—next to it. Maggie parked her bike outside, hung her helmet from the handlebar, and motioned them to the door. She bounded up the few steps, followed closely by her friends.

"Charlene, you here?"

After the bright sunshine, it took a moment for the girls to properly see the interior of the building. Inside, it was cooler and smelled, of course, like fish. A girl their age with short brown hair stood behind a large tank of lobsters and a glass case with fresh fish on ice. Maggie ran to her. "I couldn't wait to introduce you! These are the friends I've been telling you about. Vicky's the one with the long hair; Christie's the one with short. Very easy to tell apart." Maggie was bubbling over.

"Nice to meet you," Charlene said, stepping to the front of the store. Christie and Vicky returned her greeting, and Charlene walked back behind the counter, where she had been cleaning a huge halibut. Christie noticed Charlene did not seem to be as excited as Maggie was, something that was totally escaping Maggie herself in her enthusiasm. She was proposing all sorts of things for them to do together.

"Is your day off still Thursday? Maybe we can get Mom to give us extra time then. I want to see if we can get someone to take us out to Blackberry—it's this perfect little island where we can find lots of sand dollars. It's got a beautiful white sandy beach that stretches almost the whole length of the shore. And even though it is kind of tacky and super-crowded in the summer, we *have* to go up to Bar Harbor!"

"I'm not sure what my day is going to be," Charlene said. "It's really busy here." Vicky looked around. The only thing moving was a fly on its way to join the carcasses of its relatives on a long strip of flypaper twirling slightly in the air coming through the screen door. Charlene caught her gaze and flushed.

"Right now, there's a lull. You should be here when the windjammer cruise boats come in. Plus, all the summer people want everything at the same time."

The door opened behind them and the girls moved over. The flypaper spiraled over their heads.

"We have to have that for the fish," Charlene told them. She sounded annoyed. "I'm sorry, but I have to get back to work. Can I help you?"

"I'm looking for the post office," an elderly man replied. "I seem to have made a wrong turn."

"Nice to meet you," Christie said hurriedly. Vicky smiled at Charlene and waved. They went out to their bikes, expecting Maggie to follow, but Maggie was busy giving the man directions. The moment he'd spoken, she'd jumped in. "Oh, you certainly did take a wrong turn. You go back up the hill, take a left, then a right when you come to Main Street. There's even a sign that says Main Street."

He thanked her and left. The girls saw him get into his car, an old Chevrolet, then heard Charlene's unmistakable Maine accent take Maggie to task. "I think I know how to give directions, Maggie Porter, and what do you mean, 'even a sign.' We may not be Aleford, Massachusetts, but we do have street signs."

"Charlene, don't get ticked off. I was just trying to help, and you know as well as I do that we only have a few signs, and getting those was a battle at town meeting. Remember how we laughed when we heard about it? Milly Sanford saying she didn't need a sign to tell her where she'd lived all her life. What's going on with you?"

"Nothing's going on with me. Now, I *do* have work, and you shouldn't be keeping your friends waiting."

Maggie came out of the store, her cheeks blazing. She didn't say a word.

About a half a mile out of town, she told them they'd better hurry. She had to help set the tables for dinner.

"We'll help you. That's what we're here for," Vicky said.

"No, it's my job. You'll be doing enough. I'm sorry, Christie," she apologized. "No swim today. The ride took longer—"

"That's okay. We just got here. There will be plenty of time for everything." She wished Maggie would talk about the conversation with Charlene they'd overheard; maybe she would after dinner.

Maggie was adamant about not wanting any help. Vicky and Christie went to sit in the gazebo in the garden. Vicky had her sketch pad. She'd brought her watercolors, too. Everywhere she looked made her want to reach for a brush or a pencil. Christie had a book, the latest Mary Higgins Clark, and the two girls were pleasantly engaged when they heard voices on the path leading to the beach. Whining voices.

"But Mummy, all the good people were just starting to arrive. I don't understand why we had to leave Newport for this poky little place. There's absolutely nothing to do!"

"Nonsense. You have your boat to sail, and Daddy needs someone to play golf with. Besides, I want you to soak up the atmosphere of this darling, darling inn. Roots, think roots."

Vicky and Christie had covered their mouths with their hands. They were very close to revealing their presence with uncontrollable giggles.

"Still," the younger voice sounded pouty, "it's my honeymoon, and I should think I could do what I want."

"Now, angel, I know it's your honeymoon, but you and Chad can go wherever you want later. Maybe a run to the Vineyard. Daddy and I would adore to rent a place for you there."

"Well, maybe." "Angel" 's voice was suddenly calculating instead of whining. She had her mother where she wanted her and was out to get whatever she could. "I'll need some new things. That crowd has seen every old rag I own."

"Of course, Bobbie, dear. Goodness, look at the time! Let's run along and change. We don't want to be late for drinkies, do we?"

"Bobbie, dear" was still miffed. "You know we actually got here yesterday, a day early, and Chad said why don't we come for dinner and surprise them, but I said no. We had to refuel in Green Harbor anyway this morning, so we anchored, took the dinghy, and went to that place on the mainland—you know, with the good steaks—and sailed to the inn this afternoon."

If she was trying to hurt her mother's feelings, she failed.

"Whatever makes you happy, but don't tell Daddy—he might think you didn't want to see him, and you know how he gets."

"It wasn't Daddy. . . ." Bobbie continued to try to find a chink in her mother's armor.

The voices grew fainter and finally ceased completely. The two girls burst into helpless laughter.

"Yuck!" Vicky said. "Maggie was right. It is to gag. 'Drinkies'!" she shrieked.

" 'Roots, think roots'—whatever that means," Christie said, wiping away the tears of laughter streaming down her face. "When Maggie grows up, she can put them all in a book. I can't wait to see what they look like."

"I'll bet you a quarter that Bobbie is a perfect size six, very perky, tan, with a blond or light brown pageboy. Her mother may have been a six once but is more like a sixteen now, with the same color hair, except it doesn't move, even in the strongest wind.

42

And 'Daddy' probably wears those funny pants—you know the ones, with things like whales embroidered on them, or else madras ones. From the sound of it, they all deserve each other!"

"Okay, I'll take the bet, even though I'm sure I'm going to lose. We'll peek at them from the kitchen during dinner. Now I feel like taking a walk. Do you want to come?"

"I'm going to try to finish this sketch. See you later."

Christie left her book with Vicky and decided to go back down to the beach for her walk. She'd spotted some big rocks, perfect for climbing, and thought she might get a good view toward the north. Maggie said on clear days, you could see Mount Cadillac, the large mountain on Mount Desert Island, where Bar Harbor was. She set out. Soon her pockets were heavy with scallop shells, a few shells that looked liked tiny slippers with rounded soles, and some kind of large white spiral snail shells. Maggie would tell her the names. She climbed over the rocks and found herself on a small sandy beach. There were more rocks on the other side and she climbed those. The gulls had been using these for their picnics. The large, flat granite surfaces were covered with broken mussel shells and the remains of sea urchins. Christie watched one enormous gray-and-white bird hover in the air, drop its prey, and then swoop down to eat the mussel before diving back into the ocean for more. There was so much to see. The tide was rising, but she noted the spot so she could return when it was low and find out what kind of creatures lived in the tide pools.

Just as she was about to jump down to another small stretch of sand, she noticed a flight of concrete stairs and a railing. It must be another way back to the inn, she decided, and turned to follow it. It led up the cliff, then joined a well-worn path through a large meadow filled with wildflowers and tiny wild strawberries—*fraises des bois,* she remembered from French. She stopped to eat a few, warm from the sun, and vowed to come back with a container and the others to help pick. If they got enough, they could have more shortcake or maybe make jam. It was fun to think of all these projects.

At the end of the meadow, she was surprised to see another, shorter flight of stairs. This was curious. Christie climbed to the top and gasped.

There in the middle of a wide terrace was a beautiful pool, complete with diving board. Its turquoise water beckoned to her. It was too much to bear. She knew she wasn't on the Porters' property, yet the sight of the board—even a low one—after so many days without diving called to her as irresistibly as the Sirens had to Ulysses' sailors. Quickly, she slipped off her sandals, shorts, and shirt. There was no house in sight. It must be behind the trees farther up. Just one dive. That was all, she promised herself. And it wasn't swimming in the ocean, which was what she'd promised the Porters not to do. This was totally safe. She approached the board, enjoying the feel under her feet. She took three steps, then drove both arms and one leg into the air, coming down into a perfect forward dive. She hit the water without a ripple and felt a rush of excitement. It was as if she hadn't done a dive in years. She swam quickly out of the pool and, forgetting all her good resolutions, did several more dives.

"Young lady, what do you think you're doing! Come over here!"

Christie swan to the side and got out. An older woman with a sturdy cane was standing at the edge of the pool.

"Can't talk, eh! Now, how did you get here!" She pounded her cane on the cement for emphasis.

Careful not to drip on her, Christie grabbed her shirt and shorts, pulling them on over her wet under-wear. As she struggled into them, she apologized profusely.

"I'm terribly, terribly sorry. Please believe me. I've never done anything like this before. I know I must be trespassing."

"Indeed you are," the woman said.

"It's just that I came up the steps from the meadow, saw the board, and I couldn't stay away. I'm a diver." Christie had run out of excuses and stood awkwardly before the woman. She shoved her feet into her sandals.

"Probably a good one, from what I saw." It was a statement, and the woman didn't seem to expect a reply. It was also a compliment.

Christie walked closer to her. She extended her hand. "My name is Christie Montgomery. I'm from Boston and I'm visiting my friend Maggie Porter, whose parents own the Blue Heron Inn."

"The inn!" The woman reacted as if Christie had said they owned some sort of den of iniquity. She had taken Christie's hand and tightened her grip. It was amazing how strong she was for an old lady, a bent-over, thin old lady.

"Let's see, Miss Christie Montgomery. I'll make a deal with you. I know what it's like to want to do something so much that you'll even come close to breaking a law to do it—yes, trespassing is against the law. This is private property. You may come here to practice, but you can't tell a single soul. If you do—and I'll know—the deal's off."

Christie thought for a moment. She didn't like the idea of keeping a secret from Maggie and Vicky, let alone Mr. and Mrs. Porter. But she also thought about not diving, knowing the pool was here—and she wanted to find out more about this woman. Who was she?

"All right," she said. "I won't tell."

"Now get going. You don't want to be late for those fancy dinners they have over there," the woman said in a bitter voice. Christie waved to her from the top of the stairs and ran down to the beach. Halfway there, she realized she hadn't asked the woman her name. Well, that much she could find out at the inn. She thought of Roberta St. Clair and her mother, Lucinda Bishop; the woman with red hair from the ferry; Sybil Corcoran and her mouse; Charlene and the change in her friendship with Maggie; and now this. So much had happened since she'd arrived on the island, it was hard to keep it all straight.

Dinner had already started when she entered the kitchen; she had stopped to dry her hair and change clothes. Guests were beginning to dig into their main course, a creamy beef Stroganoff over basmati rice.

"What in tarnation!" The loud exclamation reached into the kitchen. Mrs. Porter had been sitting on one of the high kitchen stools. She ran full speed into the dining room for the second time that day. Her husband, who had spent the afternoon taking some guests for a sail to Vinalhaven, followed his wife. Christie & Company pulled up the rear.

"Ice water! Ice water! My mouth is burning up, I'm being poisoned!" cried one woman. Maggie dashed back into the kitchen and returned with a pitcher.

"What could be happening?" Vicky asked. The dining room was quite a sight. Guests were fanning their mouths and gulping down all the water in sight. Maggie and her parents raced into the kitchen for more.

"Is something wrong with the food?" Vicky called to Maggie in passing.

"There can't be. I tasted it myself before Mom served it out on the plates. It was delicious."

Mrs. Porter dashed past the girls, who followed her into the kitchen for more water, too. She grabbed the tin of paprika that Maggie had fetched from the pantry earlier. Maggie had given a liberal shake over each plate before it went out, per her mother's instructions. Mrs. Porter shook some of the red powder into the palm of her hand and tasted it.

"Cayenne pepper," she gasped, heading for the sink and a glass of water. "Somebody switched them!"

❖Chapter Four

FORTUNATELY, ONLY A FEW OF THE GUESTS had tasted the Stroganoff. Unfortunately, one of them was Sybil Corcoran. Mrs. Porter threw some emergency lasagna into the microwave and made a quick switch from spiced poached pears to sorbet for dessert. By that time, everyone seemed to have forgotten the incident. Everyone except Sybil Corcoran. She had immediately stormed out of the dining room, followed by her nephew, Paul, carrying a large pitcher of ice water and a glass.

"I must lie down after this horrible, horrible day!" They could hear her voice continuing to complain all the way to her room upstairs. Paul returned, looking sheepish, as usual. He bolted his dinner and left before dessert, presumably for some writing—and some peace.

An hour later, Sybil Corcoran appeared in the kitchen and imperiously demanded something on a tray—"Soothing, mind you. My tongue is very sensitive"—then left.

"You know it wasn't me, don't you, Mom?" Maggie asked anxiously after Sybil's second dramatic exit.

Both the in and out doors had been flung rather than pushed.

"Of course it wasn't you!" Julia Porter replied a bit shortly. She was eager to get this "horrible, horrible day" over and knew she should take the time to soothe her daughter's fears, but there was a tray to fix and guests waiting for coffee in the living room. Mr. Porter was busy pouring after-dinner drinks, on the house tonight. Maggie certainly knew how to pick her moments.

"But I'm the one who shook it all over the plates, so in a court of law, I'd probably be guilty." Maggie couldn't let it alone.

"Oh, Maggie, enough. I told you to do it, so in that court, I'd be convicted, too. Now let's just forget about the whole thing."

"Still, how did the cans get confused? The paprika was brand-new. Should we notify the company?"

"Maggie!"

"Okay, okay," Maggie mumbled miserably. Her two friends were looking at her, their eyes full of sympathy.

The detective regarded her sorrowfully. He really wanted to believe the dame. She was a looker, and had brains to match. "Wish I could buy that you didn't know there was arsenic in the tooth-powder can, but I'm going to have to book you."

"Why would I want to kill my own mother! She was everything to me. I've nursed her for years. Someone else must have switched the cans!"

She had been tied to her ailing mother and this

49

house for her whole life. Now she was facing another kind of prison. Arsenic! Where could it have come from? They had few visitors. Who made the switch? She let her head fall forward as the detective snapped the cuffs around her slender wrists. Her shining tresses covered her face. She didn't want him to see that her eyes were brimming with tears and her ruby lips were trembling.

If it hadn't been Maggie, who could it have been?

The outside kitchen door slammed.

It was Willy.

"Any leftovers? George and me are starving."

Maggie's eyes narrowed. "Where have you been?" she asked accusingly. His earlier words echoed in her mind. "Just you wait!" he'd said that morning. Willy was well known for his pranks, but switching the spices was going too far. "And it's George and I," she added in an unconscious imitation of her mother. Willy ignored the grammar lesson.

"After you and your snooty friends wouldn't take *I* to Green Harbor, *me* went with George in his boat to the mainland for a part for the lawn mower. It was choppy coming back. That's what took so long. But Mom knew. We called her on the CB."

Maggie flushed. She was dying to go out in George's boat. Last summer, he'd asked her often, and she'd even helped him with his lobster traps occasionally. It was hard work hauling while he maneuvered the boat, but she'd loved being out on the water in the early morning. Loved being just the two of them. Yet this summer, he hadn't said anything to her about going out. He hadn't said anything much at all, and she'd been tongue-tied every time she'd seen him. Tongue! She returned to the business at hand.

"And I suppose you don't know anything about a certain paprika can!"

Willy pointed his finger at his head and made a few circles.

"My sister gets crazier and crazier every day," he said smugly to George, who was doing a good job of blending in with the woodwork.

Maggie blew up.

"I hate you, Willy! And you are in deep, deep trouble. Someone could have gotten very sick from that pepper!"

"Maggie, stop it!" Mrs. Porter put her hands on Maggie's shoulders. "Willy doesn't even know what happened, and he would no more try to hurt anyone than, say, I would."

Maggie noticed she didn't say Maggie's name. She hated both of them at the moment. Hated herself, too. George would never ask her to go out in the boat. He must think she was a total jerk.

Vicky came to the rescue. She gave George and Willy a big smile. "You must think you've walked into the twilight zone, and in a way, today really has been far-out." She proceeded to tell them about the Towering Inferno Stroganoff and mentioned the mouse to George.

"Willy told me," he said. "Sorry I missed it," he added with a grin.

No wonder Maggie has a crush on him, Vicky

thought. George Sanford was tall and lanky. His thick blond hair was cut short and he was tan. Vicky liked his eyes—deep brown, and at the moment they were merry. Then there was that voice. She'd had a hard time at first understanding what George's father, Darnell, was saying to them as they drove from the ferry to the inn. George's accent was as far Down East as his father's, but less blurred. It was possible to recognize each word.

Maggie watched Vicky and envied the ease she had around boys. They'd talked about it at school. Christie fell somewhere between the other two—not so shy as Maggie, but not as confident as Vicky. Basically, Vicky's attitude was, What's the big deal? Maggie did have a sneaking suspicion, though, that if Vicky ever fell hard for someone, she might not be so together.

Maggie started to nibble her thumbnail. Christie moved next to her. "How much longer do you have to stick around? Maybe we can go for a walk on the beach."

"Great idea. I'll ask." Maggie's hand came quickly away from her mouth.

Her mother was busy with Ms. Corcoran's tray. It looked pretty with a single rose in a bud vase. She'd made some sandwiches and was filling a thermos with cold carrot soup.

"Do you want me to bring the tray up?" Maggie asked. "It looks very appetizing. And no mice or spice."

Her mother laughed. The whole room suddenly seemed more normal and the tension disappeared.

"Oh, Mags, 'mice and spice'—I have the feeli
thing new has been added to our family jo]

"Mice and Spice–it sounds like a name fc
fume," Christie offered.

"Or desserts for cats," Willy said.

"A friend of mine up to Green Harbor has a cat
that gets whipped cream from a can every night,"
George told them. "Did it a few times, and the cat
can't do without it now."

This caused more laughter.

"I'll take the tray. Why don't you run along with
your friends? Willy and George can eat when I come
back," Mrs. Porter said.

"Thanks, Mom, we will. But I can warm up some
Stroganoff and rice for them—no paprika." Maggie
thought quickly. Maybe Willy would want to watch
some TV or something and George would go to the
beach with them.

"No, I insist. You've worked long enough. I'm sure
the two boys won't mind waiting a minute."

There was nothing to do except leave. Once again,
Mom didn't get the message.

"Why don't you come down to the beach when
you're finished, George? I want to hear about this
boat of yours," Vicky said.

She made it seem so simple. Maggie sighed again.
Maybe Vicky could give her some lessons. But in her
heart of hearts, she didn't think it would help. She'd
still be Maggie the giraffe with glasses, a retainer on
her teeth, and too-curly hair.

Down on the beach, the inn looked like an immense
Japanese lantern glowing high above them through

the trees. There was a good breeze and the water was spraying against the rocks. The girls had brought their flashlights. Vicky shone hers out across the cove. The straight beam rippled across the surface. It would still have been light when George and Willy had arrived at Sanford Cove, but Vicky wouldn't like being out on the sea anytime it was stirred up this way. She could actually see whitecaps in her flashlight beam!

The three girls sat in companionable silence until it was broken by Vicky, as usual. She had told them when they'd first met that keeping her mouth shut was not a trick she'd mastered.

"So, it looks like we have to get busy," she said emphatically.

"Busy?" Maggie was occupied with a moonlit sail in her head.

Christie nodded. She knew what Vicky was thinking. "Absolutely. 'Mice and spice' is pretty funny, but a dead rodent in your purse and food tampering aren't. Someone at the inn has a very twisted sense of humor, and we need to find out who before Sybil Corcoran writes that article."

"You mean you guys don't think it's Willy?" Maggie was stunned.

"Do you?" Vicky asked.

Maggie paused to consider the question. "I guess I want to. I mean, he's such a pain, but it's true I can't believe even Willy would do stuff that would hurt other people—and the inn."

"All right, so let's go to work, Christie and Company." Vicky wished she'd brought her sketchbook so they could write things down.

"Starting with the mouse. Who has access to Sybil's room? I know that's disrespectful, but I can't keep calling her Sybil Corcoran. Too much of a mouthful. And is it Mrs., Miss, or Ms.? She has a rock the size of Gibralter on her ring finger, but there's no wedding band. I wonder how many karats it is. Could be a fake, though."

"Stick to the subject, Vic," Christie advised, although she was amused, as usual, by Vicky's tangents.

"She certainly didn't put the mouse in herself, and probably she looked in her bag this morning, so it had to have been done after she went into the dining room," Maggie reasoned.

"She was reading the paper on the porch. Your nice mother had brought her a cup of coffee. I remember noticing that she'd left the purse on her chair at the table in the dining room where she sits. She dumped it down with her hat. I noticed because the purse is one of those leather Coach saddlebags. They cost a fortune," Vicky said enviously.

"Looks like our little early bird got a worm," Maggie teased. "Now we can try to figure who was around—and what do you mean, 'nice mother'?"

"She is nice, Mags. Other people's mothers always are," Vicky said loftily. She spoke lightly, but she had enjoyed her time alone with Mrs. Porter and hoped she'd have more opportunities. Maybe by the end of her stay at the Blue Heron, more mysteries than the one they were talking about would be solved—

namely, the mystery of why Vicky's own mother was so distant. The change had been gradual. Each year, the space between them grew and the mother she had enjoyed as a younger child, the mother who played games with her, the mother she had confided everything in, seemed less real and more like a person Vicky had imagined.

"Besides the guests, who's at the inn that early in the morning?" Christie asked Maggie.

"Darnell, George, and sometimes other people working on the grounds. Malvina and usually one or more of her staff, but they were doing the laundry in the barn," she answered.

The inn had an old barn—all that was left of the farm that predated the big house. The Porters had converted it into a laundry room, workshop, storage area, and garage.

"Any of them could have come into the dining room without arousing suspicion," Vicky commented. "Your mother and I were setting up the buffet, but there were times when we were both in the kitchen."

"So far, we haven't eliminated anybody except us, Willy, and Sybil." Maggie summed things up. "We can eliminate the same people, minus Sybil, for the paprika. But it's hard to believe she'd take a bite of something she knew was going to taste so bogus."

"An old trick," Christie said, "Let yourself get poisoned along with the victim, just not lethally, of course."

Maggie nodded. Titles of books were leaping to mind. She was still wearing her dagger shirt. Tomorrow, she'd wear the blue one from a Texas bookstore

with the Dorothy Sayers quotation on front: SUSPECT
EVERYBODY.

"What's bogus?" It was George; blessedly, Willy
wasn't tagging along. George looked at Maggie and
smiled. "Willy is practicing knot tying and needs lots
of light. I told him he has to know these things if he
wants to keep going out on the water with me."

Maggie felt better than she had all day.

"We're talking about who could have switched the
spices—and put the dead mouse in the purse."

"What makes you think it's the same person?"

"Same juvenile mentality and too much of a coincidence, both things occurring on the same day."

Although she was sure Maggie would have liked to
continue the conversation solo, Vicky jumped in. "It
was a new tin of paprika, right? So anyone could
have put it there and waited for your mother to get
to it."

"Or emptied a lot out of the old tin. Mom did say
she seemed to be using an unusually large amount
lately when we were getting dinner ready."

"You guys sound like the real thing—Hercule
Poirot or whatever." George had read some of Maggie's mysteries and his tone was admiring. "We don't
have too many mysteries here on Little Bittern. No
police, either. Don't need them. Everybody knows everybody else. You wait. This will get straightened
out. Nobody can keep a secret for long."

Christie had been sitting looking at the star-filled
sky and feeling increasingly uneasy. It wasn't just
the dirty tricks. It was her own secret—the secret
pool and the old lady. Maybe George was right. She

certainly wanted to blurt it out. but if she did, that would mean no diving. She pressed her lips together.

After talking a while longer, George stood up and stretched. "I've got to get home. I didn't tell Dad I'd be late. Besides, I've got to check my traps before work tomorrow."

Maggie waited for an invitation, then decided he wouldn't want to ask only her, and he couldn't take all of them in his small boat. This had to be it. After smiling at her the way he had, she was sure things were still the same as they'd always been. She'd been imagining things—as usual.

George lived close to the inn, and he took off down the drive, running easily and steadily. Christie & Company started for their own quarters, when they were stopped by the sound of a loud voice on the inn's front lawn.

"He'll never be a businessman, this guy Porter."

With one accord, the three ducked down behind the nearest bushes.

"It's Hap Hotchkiss," Maggie whispered.

The other person started talking. "You know these artistic types, Hap. Writers! Heads in the clouds."

"And loathsome Uncle Bob," Maggie added, identifying the second speaker.

"Heard there were troubles at mealtimes today." Hap chuckled. "Lady found a mouse dead as a doornail in her purse!"

"Almost put me off my waffles. I mean, I was laughing so hard!"

Vicky pointed her finger down her throat. Both

men were smoking cigars, so gagging was very nearly true.

"And how did it go at dinner?"

"Lucky thing Lucinda, the kids, and I hadn't started eating. People who did had steam pouring out of their ears."

Maggie was startled by the way the two men were talking—confidently, as if they were old friends, partners of some kind.

Partners in crime?

❖ Chapter Five

"**B**UT DAD, IT WAS THE *WAY* THEY WERE saying things, not so much *what* they said," Maggie protested.

"Mags, my love, I treasure your wonderful imagination, but this time you have gone way, way overboard."

Maggie and her father were in the boathouse. He was applying a second coat of paint to a canoe he'd recently repaired. There was a smudge of red paint on the tip of his nose. Maggie decided not to tell him.

"At least promise me that you'll be on the lookout for any stuff going on between them."

"I promise." Her father smiled good-naturedly at his very serious daughter.

"Although," Ned Porter continued, "I have no idea what kind of 'stuff' I should be looking for. The two men are friends. Am I supposed to plant myself between them whenever I see them together?"

Her father was so exasperating—he just didn't get it. Maybe Bob Bishop was right and Dad did have his head too high in the clouds to be a businessman. She should probably be telling all this to her mother, but that would mean having to listen to Mom's un-abridged version of Maggie's father's comment on Maggie's imagination. A version Maggie knew by heart.

"It wouldn't hurt." Maggie continued to prod her father. "And why are they friends? And how did they meet? On the island? It seems unlikely, and if it was off-island, where would their paths cross?"

"Sounds like the beginning of a good mystery story, but not much like real life. I'm sure they met here. Remember, Bob has been coming to the inn since be-fore we opened."

"I remember," Maggie said sarcastically, but her tone was lost on her father, who was busy cleaning the brush and humming, "Oh, What A Beautiful Mornin'."

"Now, that looks better," he said, admiring his handiwork. He glanced at his watch. "And you'd bet-ter get up to the kitchen. After yesterday, your mother did not have a good night's sleep. A word to the wise . . ."

Maggie was already out the door and climbing the steep path back to the inn. She'd set her alarm to join her father for a private chat. The last thing she wanted was to be late for breakfast duty two days in a row.

All three girls had found the conversation between Hap Hotchkiss and Robert Bishop distinctly puzzling and, taken with everything else going on, more than a little suspicious. They had once more stayed up too late talking.

Vicky had beaten Maggie to the kitchen again and

had already taken her morning shower. She was perched on a stool, busy squeezing oranges for juice and talking to Julia Porter. It was fast becoming an accepted routine. Christie arrived just after Maggie, still rubbing the sleep from her eyes. "We have *got* to stop staying up so late," she said to Maggie as she grabbed a stack of cereal bowls for the buffet.

"What do you girls have planned for today?" Mrs. Porter asked.

"It's not so much the day as the night," Maggie answered. "Could you drive us to the Fourth of July dance at the Legion Hall?"

"And how about permission to attend?"

"Oh, Mom, you know I've gone every year! Even kids Willy's age go," Maggie complained.

"I know. I just like to be asked. Of course you can go, and yes, we'll drive. I'm glad you reminded me, because Willy might like to go, too—and some of the guests."

"Me and my big mouth," Maggie fumed.

"What was that, Margaret?"

"Nothing, Mother dear." Her mother never missed anything!

"That's good. The dance starts at seven, right?"

"Yes," Maggie said. Social events on the island started early and ended early. People were on a different schedule from the mainland, different rhythms.

After breakfast, the girls tidied their cabin and headed back to the shore.

"So, what is this dance all about?" Vicky asked. She wanted plenty of time to figure out what to wear.

"There are dances at the hall most Saturday nights during the summer, and everybody goes. It's kind of nice, because you never feel left out. There's always someone to talk to, even if you're not dancing."

"You mean not like that first horrible dance at Cabot with the Mansfield Hill boys when nobody danced until almost the end, after the chaperones forced people."

Maggie still cringed when she recalled trying to appear completely invisible at said dance.

"No, not like that! Maybe because it's all ages—and all kinds of music. Tonight, it's this group from Stonington—the Melodic Mariners."

"Sounds cool, very nautical," Christie said. "What do you want to do this morning?"

She couldn't help blushing. What she wanted to do was to sneak over to the pool. Why, oh why, had the owner sworn her to secrecy? It was time to find out more about the cantankerous old lady from Maggie. "Maybe we could explore the shore around here, possibly take a dip. I don't see any signs of neighbors." Christie looked down the beach, "Do you have any?"

Vicky had made a face at the word *dip,* but she followed up on the neighbors question.

"Yeah, who else lives here, Maggie?"

"If you keep walking around the point in that direction"—Maggie gestured to her left—"eventually you'll get to where Darnell and George and a whole lot of other Sanfords live. It's called Sanford Cove, in fact. Their lobster boats are moored there—it's like a little village."

"You've never mentioned George's mother. What about her?" Vicky asked.

"She died when George was born. Darnell, and the entire Sanford clan, has raised George. He only mentioned her to me once. I was reading and he told me his mother had been a great reader."

Christie's face darkened. "Poor George," she said softly. "It was bad enough for me. But never to have known your mother. No memories. Nothing except what other people tell you." Her memories of her mother were like a patchwork quilt. Christie constantly looked at each tiny square of cloth that made up the pattern, pulling the whole thing tightly around her for comfort—and protection.

Maggie and Vicky nodded. The girls were silent for a moment, then Vicky broke in.

"What happens if you walk the other way, to the right?" she asked. Christie picked up a stone and appeared to be examining the pockmarked pattern the tides had made in the granite's surface. She was all ears, and it could just as well have been a diamond in her tight grip.

"Oh, that's where old Caroline Griffith lives. She's a recluse and supposed to be kind of weird. I've never seen her, but Malvina says local people give her a wide berth. They think she's a kind of witch, and the island is not a superstitious place. Some old story about a relative—a girl anyway—who disappeared in the night. We'll have to ask Malvina or Charlene more about it."

"Do they think she's dangerous?" Christie asked

incredulously. Caroline Griffith had seemed eccentric, maybe, but not harmful.

"Not exactly. You just don't want to annoy her, I guess, or your pig might die. That kind of thing." Maggie laughed.

"What's her house like?" Christie asked.

"I've never seen it from the land, but by water, you can make out most of it. Very grand, not so old as the inn, although almost as big. Her family owned the inn at one time. It was her grandfather who built it. There are Griffiths all over these islands. Her father and his brother owned a steamship company based in Boston and New York."

"But why didn't she stay at the inn? Why did she sell?"

"Nobody had lived in the inn since the early seventies. It belonged to some kind of trust. I don't think she'd lived here since she was a child."

"But it seems strange that she would have moved to such a big house all by herself and right next door, give or take a few hundred pine trees," Christie mused.

"Another mystery." Maggie's eyes sparkled. "And George said there weren't any on this island!"

"Speaking of the boy, will he be there tonight?" Vicky asked. "And if so, I hope he has some friends."

"He usually goes to the dances." Maggie paused. "Help me pick out something to wear that won't make me look too dorky, okay?"

"Oh, Maggie!"

In the end, the friends split up, Maggie and Vicky to examine wardrobe possibilities and Christie to take a walk—a walk she knew would end up at the pool. She had her suit on under her cutoffs and shirt today. She'd even stuffed a bathing cap in her pocket so she wouldn't have to account for her hair if it hadn't dried by the time she met the others for a picnic lunch.

She retraced her steps and soon she was feeling the board beneath her toes. Climbing rocks and going up and down the paths to the beach were as good as "stairs"—an exercise the coach made them do in which they ran up and down the bleachers for what seemed like hours. Whatever she'd been doing, as well as her warm-up exercises, made her feel limber and in control. She went through a series of dives.

Breaking the surface of the water, the blue sky seemed to surround her. There were only a few wispy clouds. She began to pay attention to the smallest sounds—the birds overhead, the ocean below, the breeze, and a rustle in the bushes as a small red squirrel darted about. She took a break and lay flat on her back in the sun next to a small shed. There was a padlock on it, but it wasn't snapped shut. Probably pool supplies were kept there. The squirrel climbed to the roof, chattering at her. Her eyes drifted shut. Suddenly, she was awakened by a shadow across her face, and she sat up. It was Caroline Griffith.

The old woman didn't look particularly menacing. She was wearing a blue cotton skirt, flowered blouse, and soft yellow wool sweater. Her white hair was thick and pulled back into a French twist.

"Good morning," Christie said, then added, "thank you again for letting me use the pool."

"I've been watching you. You're quite a diver, young lady, and you stick to it. You must have done that one you were having trouble with twenty times."

"Twenty-two," Christie said. It was true. Her coach often said Christie was her own harshest judge. She wanted perfection. So much of her life was out of control. In the pool, she was mistress of her fate. She thought about explaining this, but instead she asked the old lady how long she had lived in her house. The question popped out of nowhere.

"How long? Let's see. Papa built it for us when we were married, so that would have been fifty-three years ago. We put the pool in later."

"Married, but I thought—" Christie stopped abruptly, then decided she'd better continue. She had to be honest with someone. "I didn't tell them about the pool or meeting you, but I did ask about you indirectly, so I know your name."

"This might be amusing. Why don't you come up to the house for a glass of lemonade and tell me what they're saying. I don't hear much of this sort of thing."

Christie hesitated, then, drawn by her own curiosity, followed the woman up some sloping stairs to a formal garden leading to the house.

It was smaller than the inn, but a jewel. Its white paint sparkled in the sun and it would have been at home overlooking the Mississippi. The front had a wide veranda with tall columns. The windows stretched high, as well. There was a second-story balcony.

"My husband and I took a honeymoon in New Orleans and went out the River Road. I didn't see why I couldn't have my own plantation house on the coast of Maine. I was very, very young and my husband was just a plain fool. Worse, but that's another story."

Mrs. Griffith took Christie in the back door. There was a short hallway leading to a large kitchen. A woman was working at the sink, scrubbing pots.

"We'd like some lemonade in the parlor when you have a chance, Marie."

The woman nodded.

"Marie and her husband are from Quebec. They take care of me. Better than I deserve, right, Marie?"

"Oh no, madame!" Marie's accent was strong; her protest seemed genuine. Had *she* been bewitched? Christie was beginning to doubt this whole local legend thing.

The parlor was filled with light and large arrangements of flowers. Several portraits and some landscapes hung on the walls. There was one Christie recognized immediately—the view from the front of the house.

"So, what is the island saying about me lately?"

"That you keep to yourself and it's not a good idea to make you angry." Christie thought she'd summed things up pretty well. No way was she going to mention the word *witch*.

Mrs. Griffith nodded. She seemed pleased.

"Was it a coincidence that you married someone

named Griffith and it was also your maiden name? Or did you keep your maiden name?" Christie wanted to know. She'd assumed when Maggie said that the Griffiths had built the inn that Caroline was unmarried.

"Women didn't do that sort of thing when I got married, although there were the Lucy Stoners—they kept their maiden names after marriage. I remember when one of them got a passport issued in her maiden name, Doris Fleischmann, the first woman to do so. It was big news. Now you all take it for granted."

Christie shook her head. "I don't. My friends don't, either. Things still aren't right, but they'd be a lot worse if all those women hadn't worked and fought so hard. My mother—" She choked a moment and started again. "My mother used to talk to me about it a lot."

Mrs. Griffith looked at her piercingly. "You have your secrets, too, I suspect. Anyway, mine is not very interesting. I married a distant cousin come for a summer visit—in haste, as they say, then, while repenting in leisure, grew to despise him. Eventually, he left. I don't know whether he's even still alive or not. He married again, of course. Gave some other woman a devil of a life."

"Did you have any children?"

"I *had* a child." Mrs. Griffith put a strong emphasis on the word *had.* Christie's eye filled with tears.

"I'm very sorry. . . ."

"Don't be. It wasn't my fault," Mrs. Griffith answered angrily. The white waves of hair framing her face shook. Christie decided to drop the subject and grasped for a safe topic. The paintings.

"You have some wonderful paintings." She got up and walked around, examining one in particular as Mrs. Griffith talked to Marie, who had brought the lemonade and a plate of cookies.

The painting was of a young child running through a meadow filled with daisies. The artist had captured the child's joyful expression perfectly. It was a little girl, a beautiful little girl with long red-gold curls. Was this Mrs. Griffith's daughter? Christie wondered. A daughter who had gone away? A daughter who was dead?

"Come have something to eat—Marie's sugar cookies are delicious—and tell me how they're doing at that inn."

"I think they're very successful, although some awful things have been happening lately." Christie told her about the events of the day before, but rather than commiserating, Mrs. Griffith laughed out loud.

"Serves 'em right. Never liked the idea of an inn. Papa would *not* have approved. Besides, the house never brought anyone good luck."

"But the Porters are my friends, and it's horrible for them."

"Oh pish. If they can't take a few upsets, they shouldn't be in business."

Christie had never heard anyone say this particular word outside of books. She decided not to protest anymore.

"I have to go. They'll be wondering where I am." She wanted to ask what was unlucky about the house—which was now the inn—but it was getting very late.

"Suit yourself. The pool's here if you want it." Mrs. Griffith raised her hand dismissively.

"Don't you use it yourself?"

"Can't stand pools. When I used to swim, I swam right in the cove. Papa used to lead us in before breakfast every morning."

"Then why did you build the pool?"

"You ask too many questions. Now, be on your way. I'm tired." It was as if a curtain had closed over the old woman's face. Christie left quickly.

It took Vicky Lee's eyes a few moments to adjust to the dimly lit interior of Little Bittern's Legion Hall, a barnlike wooden building. Outside, it had still been light. A large ball with tiny mirrors pasted on it revolved slowly above the dancers' heads, sending bright patterns all over the room. She stretched her arm out and watched the light flicker across the sleeve of the gauzy white shirt she was wearing, the long tails tied at her waist. Underneath was a shiny black T-shirt that just reached the top of her pleated short black skirt. She'd added her silver bracelets and let her hair hang loose. She liked to feel it on her face as she danced, and she hoped she would be dancing. At the moment, it looked as if the entire population of the island was. The band was playing, of all things, "Twist and Shout." Little kids were vigorously grinding away alone, with one another, or with partners who looked old enough to be their grandparents.

"I really like this," she said to Maggie, who was anxiously scanning the crowd. After changing her mind innumerable times, Maggie was wearing a bright pink cropped T-shirt of Vicky's, jeans, and a denim vest.

"What? Oh yeah, the dances are great, and don't worry, they play all kinds of music."

Christie was looking around, too. She was surprised to see Marie and a man who was probably her husband in the midst of a group of people by the refreshment booth. She doubted Mrs. Griffith would be here, but she kept looking. Christie had jeans on, too, a tank top, and an oversized white tuxedo shirt, an old one of her father's she'd grabbed from the Goodwill pile. She imagined it smelled faintly of the cologne he wore, which her mother had given him each Christmas. Christie had remembered to put a bottle in his stocking this year, and he said it was his best present.

"Isn't that George and your friend Charlene?" Christie asked Maggie. "Over there by the door?"

Maggie darted away, calling over her shoulder, "Yes, come on. All the kids are there."

Vicky and Christie followed her, weaving their way among the dancers. The music had changed to the "Beer Barrel Polka." It reminded Vicky of a wedding reception, or her friend Liza's bat mitzvah party. She was willing to swear they'd be doing the bunny hop before the night was over.

Maggie was already talking to George, and she rapidly introduced her friends to everyone. A few nodded and smiled. Vicky caught only one or two names.

"Everybody get a partner for 'Achy Breaky Heart'."

The island kids paired off. One was wearing cowboy boots. Line dancing was evidently popular here, too.

"Come on, George," Charlene said.

"I promised this one to Maggie. Catch you later," he answered.

Charlene walked off angrily and Maggie felt torn. George hadn't promised her anything, and what was Charlene doing? She knew how Maggie felt about George. Maggie had confided in her all last summer. Should she follow her friend and try to find out what was going on? But George had put out his hand. She took it and went out onto the floor.

"Would you care to join them, Miss Lee?" Christie asked Vicky with mock solemnity.

"Don't mind if I do."

The familiar tune started and everybody danced. Without pause, the band went into another one.

"We were made to dance together," he whispered into his partner's ear. Her long silver gown shimmered in the moonlight. He had swept her onto the terrace, away from the crowded dance floor. It was true; their steps flowed together so perfectly that it seemed as if one person was dancing, one shadow on the ground. She let her head rest against his. "Our life will be one long dance, my darling, if you will only say the words I've been waiting to hear."

*   *   *

"Are you thirsty, Maggie?"

"Oh yes! Yes!"

"Gee," said George, "I thought I needed a Coke, but you sound like you're dying for one. Come on, let's go. I want a sandwich, too."

Slightly dazed, partly remaining in her daydream, Maggie followed George off the floor, waving to Vicky and Christie, who were still dancing.

After they got their drinks and George selected the biggest sandwich he could find, they went out to the parking lot for some air.

"I want to tell you something," George had said as they were each paying Mrs. Cousins, who was helping to run the food stand for the benefit of the Island Fishermen's Wives Association.

By the time they sat down on a rock by the cars, Maggie thought George could certainly hear her heart—it was pounding so loudly. What did he want to tell her?

"Don't think we'll have any fights tonight." He glanced at the groups scattered across the parking lot. "There're a few people I don't see. Must have gone to the mainland for some of the early Fourth of July things up to Bar Harbor." He took an enormous bite of his sandwich. Little Bittern dances sometimes resulted in high feelings and bloody noses.

Maggie waited, drank her Coke, and hoped desperately that she wouldn't burp.

"My dad isn't going to tell your parents, but I think they ought to know. If I tell you, you can tell them."

"Tell them what?" Maggie's heart sank, yet she was so curious about whatever *this* was that her disappointment was over as soon as it began. And disappointment over what? a tiny voice asked. She certainly didn't want to go steady.

"When Dad got to the inn this morning, he found a dead seagull on the front porch. The dog went for it."

"But that's not so unusual. Although having a seagull die on the porch is a bit gross. Maybe an animal left it there. Another dog."

"Wait. It's head was cut off. Cut off clean, with a knife. The only animal that could do that is a human animal."

It wasn't stopping. The bad things. The gruesome gull was meant to be seen, and if Darnell hadn't spotted it and removed it, one or more of the guests would have—and passed along the grisly news.

"Who can be doing this to us?" Maggie wondered aloud.

"The gull looked like it had been lying around a while, Dad said. Whoever did it must have found it on the beach, then cut the head. Really stank."

"I'll tell Mom and Dad, but I wish your father had said something right away. In any case, they'll check with him. They think I'm imagining all this, imagining that there's some kind of conspiracy."

"Dad doesn't want to get involved. 'It's none of our business,' he told me, but I don't want to see anything happen to the inn."

Until George said the words out loud, Maggie hadn't realized that this was her secret fear, too. So far, the incidents had been minor annoyances.

But now she was scared.

As they were going back inside, a carload of people

drove up. Drove up fast and burned rubber just in front of the door. Maggie looked to see who it was, expecting some of the older teenagers, who got their kicks this way. It was an older "teenager." A much older teenager—Bobbie's new husband, Chad St. Clair. He got out, boasting about the way he'd handled the car, a new Jeep Cherokee that the Bishops had brought over on the ferry. Bobbie got out on the other side, and people Maggie didn't recognize, all about the St. Clair's age and type, followed.

"Let's check out the local scene. Bobbie says it's a hoot. We can always go back to the boat and party some more if it's a drag."

They had obviously been partying a lot already.

"Why, it's the innkeeper's daughter." Chad made an exaggerated bow. "I thought they kept you locked in your room at night, fair maiden." His friends howled with laughter. Bobbie said, "Oh, leave her alone, Chad. She might tell her mommy and daddy on us. Are we going in or not?"

Maggie stepped back and George stepped forward. His eyes narrowed as he said in a purposefully thick Maine accent, "We don't allow alcohol on the premises here." His cheeks had flushed when he'd heard the word *hoot,* and now he was even more furious. He didn't care how many of them there were.

"Oh, how sweet. Maggie's got her own little cop. Don't worry, sonny, it's all inside us." Again the group seemed to find Chad the funniest thing since Jerry Seinfeld. They all went in, leaving Maggie and George seething.

"That jerk! They deserve each other. I can't understand how my parents can let them keep coming."

"Don't worry, Mags, before they leave Little Bittern, we'll think of something." He grinned at her, "I'd hate to think what a bucket of bait would do to the inside of that pretty new boat of theirs."

Now Maggie laughed. The bait would attract the gulls, who would be sure to leave lots of souvenirs.

Back in the hall, Vicky and Christie were talking with Maggie's island friends. The band was taking a break and there was a crowd at the refreshment counter. Maggie looked for Charlene. She needed to speak with her, but Charlene was helping to make more sandwiches. When Maggie offered her aid as well, she received a curt "No, thank you."

"Charlene, we have *got* to talk. Will you meet me outside when you're finished here?"

Charlene's mother was giving Maggie a cool stare. "I don't think that will be possible tonight, deah."

Maggie didn't take any comfort in the use of the word *dear*. On the island, it was sprinkled in conversation like salt. Now what had she done to the Compton family? She searched her memory for something she might have said or done to annoy them, but she couldn't think of a thing. What was going on? Could it have had anything to do with George turning down Charlene's offer to dance? Both mother and daughter continued to ignore her. There was nothing to do but walk away and find her friends.

The band started up again and the St. Clairs and their friends were dancing wildly and crazily all over the floor, bumping into people. Finally, they left and the whole building breathed a sigh of relief. Maggie's parents appeared soon after.

"Why couldn't they have come a few minutes earlier!" she moaned to Christie and Vicky. "If I say anything about Bobbie and Chad, they'll just say they were having a good time and that I'm blowing things out of proportion again."

"So, don't say anything. But you have to tell them about the gull on the way home. We'll back you up, and maybe George will come with us," Vicky said. As soon as Maggie had come in, she'd told the rest of Christie & Company about Darnell's grim discovery.

The Porters took time to dance. It was to a spirited rendition of the Beatles' "A Hard Day's Night" and Maggie had to suffer the embarrassment of watching her parents gyrate around the floor. They collected Willy, who had spent most of the dance looking for deposit cans in the parking lot with his friends, and started for the inn.

George did get a ride with them, and at Maggie's prodding, he told the Porters about the decapitated bird.

"It sounds nasty," Mr. Porter said, "but I still can't imagine that this has anything to do with us. Some kind of diabolical plot to close us down—that's absurd."

Maggie could see her mother's face. Her lips were shut tight and, even after her husband's comments, they didn't open in agreement or disagreement.

For once, Julia Porter wasn't saying anything.

❖Chapter Six

VICKY WAS TALKING ABOUT HER MOTHER. She had come to enjoy these prebreakfast chats with Mrs. Porter, even though her original impulse had been to avoid the shock of cold water after a three-minute shower—totally impossible.

Maggie's mother looked at the girl at her side, who was energetically rolling out dough for biscuits—a girl so different from her own little Magpie. She was willing to bet the girl had never dawdled in her life—except maybe in front of a mirror. Vicky was practical and moved swiftly, efficiently. But she doesn't have Maggie's imagination, Mrs. Porter thought fondly.

"Why can't I get her to talk to me? It's like a stone wall. The Great Wall of China," Vicky added, attempting to lighten the mood. When she started the biscuits, her face turned away from her friend's mother, Vicky had suddenly found herself blurting out all her problems with *her* mother.

"Then your mother was born in China, not Hong Kong like you?" Mrs. Porter felt she knew her daughter's friends intimately. Maggie was a gifted letter writer.

"She was sent to Hong Kong to live with relatives after her mother died. Her father died when she was a baby."

"I'm so sorry. How old was she when she left?"

"I'm not really sure. She never talks about it. My cousin Teddy is the one who told me even this much. He thought she was about eleven or twelve."

"There's no good time to lose a parent, but it's particularly difficult when you're that age—on the edge of growing up."

"I know. Look at what Christie is going through."

"Maggie's told me about it, and Christie's lucky to have such good friends. Your mother must have had good friends, and perhaps relatives she was close to, whom she had to leave far behind."

This had never occurred to Vicky. Once, she had come across an old photograph of two little girls and her mother had told her it was of herself and her cousin Chui. They were standing in a garden with their arms around each other. *Chui* meant "green jade" in Chinese, something—and someone—highly prized. Her mother hadn't known the relatives in Hong Kong, Teddy said. Vicky felt she was very close to understanding her problem. She needed to talk to Mrs. Porter some more.

"Do you think—"

There was a loud knock on the kitchen door. Mrs. Porter jumped up to answer it. No one ever knocked; they just pushed it open. In the dining room, suitcases in hand, stood two guests. They had arrived on Thursday night to spend a week. They had been staying in one of the cottages.

The man started to speak, but his wife interrupted. Her voice was shrill.

"We could overlook the mouse and the mistake with the food, but someone trying to scare us to death in the middle of the night is no laughing matter! We used the phone at the front desk to call that man from Island Transport, and he'll be here any minute to take us to the ferry. I wouldn't stay at this inn if *you* were paying *me*."

"Please, Mr. and Mrs. Logan, come in, sit down, and tell me what this is all about. Vicky, run and find Mr. Porter. He's probably in the boathouse."

Vicky ran past the irate couple.

"No, we will not sit down! I want to watch for the car," Mrs. Logan said, and folded her arms across her chest. She marched to the front of the inn and stood by the window. Her husband and Mrs. Porter followed her single file, making an uneasy and ill-assorted parade.

"My wife is not easily upset," Mr. Logan said. "Nor am I. But at around two o'clock this morning, we heard a noise, like someone moaning outside our cabin window. I turned on the light, thinking it was an injured animal, and started to go outside, when a face in one of those *Friday the Thirteenth* masks appeared. Mrs. Logan screamed and I ran out the door. Whoever it was took off into the woods. I can tell you, we didn't get much sleep after that. With no phone, we couldn't call you, and my wife didn't want me to go outside again."

"I can't tell you how sorry I am—and I *can't* imagine who it could have been," Mrs. Porter said. "A local teenager maybe, Saturday-night pre–Fourth of July high jinks. A dare." She was fumbling for words.

"Whatever it was, we are out of here. And you'd better get this mess straightened out, before you have an empty inn. We will look for your check for the full reimbursement for our stay."

"Of course, but please, won't you reconsider? Tonight there'll be room here in the main part of the inn."

Cliff Compton's ancient Ford wagon appeared. In addition to the only garage on the island, he operated a taxi service in the summer.

"Here's the man now. Let's go!" Mrs. Logan tugged at her husband's sleeve.

"It's a shame. Nice little operation you have here." He followed his wife, who was literally sprinting for the car.

Great, thought Mrs. Porter. The Logans will no sooner be on the *Miss Hattie* than Cliff will have spread the word over the entire island. But it would have gotten out anyway. Life on Little Bittern had taught her many lessons, and the island grapevine had both its good and bad points.

Ned Porter came running up the path, followed by Christie & Company on their way for breakfast detail.

"What's going on? Vicky said the Logans are in some kind of a huff." Maggie's father's voice was puzzled.

Mrs. Porter told them what had happened, then asked the girls to finish setting up the breakfast buffet and put the biscuits in the oven. She needed to be alone with her husband for a few minutes. As soon as her mother and father were out of the kitchen, Maggie turned to her friends. "I think we should help Malvina do the rooms this morning. And right after breakfast, someone needs to go out to the cabin where the Logans were staying and see if there are any clues."

"I'll go," said Christie. Neither girl needed to ask why they were going to help change sheets and put out fresh towels. They'd be looking for Jason.

"Nothing." Christie collapsed in a heap under the large oak tree in front of the inn, where the other two girls were waiting. "What about you?"

"Well, we couldn't actually rifle through people's belongings, but we did snoop around open closets and whatever was in plain sight. You can't imagine the number of cosmetics Sybil Corcoran uses—and it's all that expensive imported kind, guaranteed to make wrinkles vanish," Vicky said.

"It was also hard because Malvina was watching us. I think she got suspicious when we were such willing volunteers. She knows how much I hate making beds. Anyway, we came up with zip, too, except for some interesting impressions, as Vicky has pointed out. Sybil's nephew's room is like a monk's. He could fit all his clothes in one small suitcase. Everything was neat as a pin. No towels thrown on the bathroom floor like his aunt." Maggie had enjoyed doing the guests' rooms for a change.

"He's reading one of those thick sci-fi paperbacks.

It was the only thing on the table next to his bed. I wonder if that's what he's writing?" Vicky added.

Christie filled them in on her investigation.

"I looked all around the Logans' cottage and into the woods. No discarded masks, but somebody had definitely been standing outside the bedroom window. Several branches were broken on a bush growing underneath, although there weren't any footprints—the ground is covered with pine needles. From another broken branch I found, I'd say he, or she, ran off in the direction of the white house you told us about, not toward the inn and the road."

"That's strange. Mrs. Griffith is supposed to be kind of strange, but somehow I can't picture a little old lady getting her kicks from putting on a fright mask and looking in people's windows," Maggie said.

Christie had stammered a little when she mentioned the white house she was not supposed to know about. Her voice was firm now. "I'm sure she doesn't have anything to do with it."

The other two looked at her curiously, and she was on the point of telling all, when Willy came up.

"I didn't do it," he said belligerently, standing directly in front of the girls. "I know you're going to try to blame this on me, too, but honest, I would never do anything to drive people away. I want to run the place myself someday."

This was news to Maggie. She wasn't sure what she thought about it.

"Nobody's blaming you," Christie said. "Of course you wouldn't do such a stupid, and frightening, thing."

Maggie was about to say something along the lines of "Don't be so sure," but then a thought struck her.

"Will, don't you have one of those masks?"

"Yeah, it's in the barn in a pile of stuff I moved there when we had to get out of our rooms."

All three jumped up at the same time and headed for the barn, Willy running behind them, calling, "Hey, wait for me!"

There were several open cartons overflowing with Willy's treasures.

"I put it in this one with some other Halloween things." Willy started tossing various articles onto the barn floor. Vicky picked up a vampire cape and twirled around, "My, vhat a lovely neck you have," she said in her best Transylvanian accent.

"It's not here." Willy sounded definite.

"Are you sure? Maybe you put it in one of the other boxes."

They emptied all of them and searched the barn. No mask.

"I've got to tell Mom and Dad!" Willy started to leave the barn.

"Wait," Maggie said. At this point, her parents were harried—and skeptical. "Let's do a little sleuthing on our own first. You can help." That should do it, she thought. It did. Willy immediately sat down.

"Okay." He made a zipping motion across his mouth. "Now what?"

"Well, the missing mask proves it was someone from the Blue Heron," Vicky reasoned.

Christie took the thought one step further. "A

guest or somebody who works here. Somebody who could come into the barn and poke around."

Maggie's brow was furrowed. If things continued the way they were headed, she was going to need a truckload of Sybil Corcoran's wrinkle cream.

"What are you guys doing sitting around in here on a beautiful day like this? I've been looking everywhere for you." It was Mr. Porter. He was dressed in his sailing uniform—Top-Siders, rolled-up jeans, a shirt with the name of the boat, *Gentle Julia,* embroidered over the pocket, and his ancient salt-stained white canvas sailing hat.

"Since the Logans are gone, I think I can squeeze the four of you on the boat today. That is, if you'd like to come."

"Oh, Dad, we'd love to. I mean"—Maggie turned to her friends—"would you like to go sailing?"

Christie nodded enthusiastically.

"As the lady said, we'd love to." Vicky smiled at Mr. Porter. She'd taken a look at the water today and it was calm and smooth, no squalls on the horizon.

"I thought we'd go over to Stonington. That's the largest town on Deer Isle. It's a nice run and we can go ashore. There are some galleries and gift shops people like to explore. Your mother is packing a lunch and we'll leave when she's finished, so skedaddle."

"I like your father," Christie said back in their cabin as the girls grabbed sunblock, caps, and jackets—it could get cool very suddenly on the water, Maggie cautioned.

"I like him, too. It's Mom I'm working on," Maggie said ruefully.

"It's totally normal for girls our age not to get along with their mothers perfectly. Isn't that what all the books say—that we're testing our independence? Your mother at least talks to you and you *know* she loves you. Why don't you try telling her how you feel?" Vicky wished she could follow her own good advice.

"Maybe you're right," Maggie said cheerfully, "but not today. We're going boatin'."

As they were leaving the cabin, Christie tripped on an uneven board and the chair she grabbed to avoid falling knocked over one of the stacks of pictures leaning against the wall.

"Way to go, Christie," she said, and started to put the pile back. She hoped none of the frames had been chipped.

None had, but she stopped openmouthed as she came to a portrait photograph of a young woman. It had been hand-tinted and the woman was wearing a dark green dress with a beautiful lace collar. It wasn't the dress she noticed, though. It was the face and the hair—the red hair. The picture looked exactly like the woman on the ferry, although much younger of course. Except it couldn't be. This photo would have been taken before that woman was even born. She turned it over to look for a name or date. There was nothing on it. Maybe it was written on the back, inside the frame.

"What is it? What did you find?" Maggie and Vicky peered over her shoulder.

"I've seen her somewhere. I know. On the landing, only that woman was older," Maggie said.

Christie hastily put the rest of the pictures against the wall and left with the others, resolving to open the back of the photograph the first chance she got.

"Look, quick—it's a seal! Oh, there are lots of them!" Vicky pointed excitedly to a ledge as the boat sailed by.

Christie laughed. "Look at their faces! They're so cute!"

Maggie was looking at her father's face. While not bearing much resemblance to the harbor seals—and they *were* cute—he looked as happy as one with a herring in its mouth. Ned Porter's thirty-six-foot Sabre was his pride and joy. He liked nothing better than to take people out for a sail. Maggie was happy, too. It was a perfect Maine day, which meant the sky, which always seemed endless when you were on the water, was blue, the sun bright, and the breeze enough to fill the sails but not cause swells. The sloop almost seemed to be sailing herself today, effortlessly catching the wind and slicing through the deep cerulean waters of Penobscot Bay. Maggie leaned back and looked straight up at the mast.

"It's a new record! These Cup Races are always full of surprises, and this one will go down in history. The youngest skipper and her female crew—complete unknowns until now!" The announcer's voice was filled with excitement. "Yes, ladies and gentlemen, it's official. They've crossed the line!" Captain Margaret

Porter allowed herself a weary smile as her crew flashed V for Victory signs at her. They still had to sail into port. All those hours of training, raising money to outfit the boat, overriding the skepticism of some of her relatives. Victory. Yes, it was sweet. But she couldn't have done it without her friends.

Maggie dozed off into a half sleep, soon disturbed by the voices of two of the other passengers—Lucinda Bishop and Sybil Corcoran.

Another couple had cut short their stay at the Blue Heron, telling Mrs. Porter that they had changed their plans and wanted to be on the mainland for the Fourth of July celebrations, but no one was fooled. The Bishops had taken their places on the boat. Maggie wondered why they weren't sailing with their obnoxious daughter and son-in-law, and soon she heard the answer.

"Bobbie and Chad are pooped," Mrs. Bishop was telling Sybil. "You know how stressful a wedding is, what with all the preparations."

Maggie opened her eyes a slit. Her friends were sitting with Willy at the bow. Mr. Bishop and her father were chatting amiably at the helm. Uncle Bob was an avid sailor, too. Sybil Corcoran looked bored.

"Whatever," the magazine editor said in response to Mrs. Bishop's prattling.

"Anyway, they were going to take us over to Stonington. A dear, dear friend has an exhibit at one of the galleries there. But I told them to rest. They didn't even come down to breakfast."

Maggie wasn't surprised. And the reason the St.

Clairs were "pooped" had nothing to do with their wedding. More likely, it was the amount of alcohol they'd had the night before. She barely repressed a shudder, conjuring up a vivid mental image of the two of them heaving in the bushes. Probably their idea of matrimonial bliss. What idiots! She closed her eyes completely, all the better to hear. Let them think she was asleep.

"Such a quaint inn, the Blue Heron. You know my husband and I virtually set it up for them; then our work was done and we backed off. Unfortunately, the Porters, dears that they are, don't seem to be . . . well, shall we say in touch with their guests' needs?"

Sybil Corcoran showed a spark of interest. "What do you mean?"

"There was the mouse, as you know—and I have to say, I thought you were a very courageous woman—then the food, and now people leaving in droves because of some sort of masked figure appearing at windows in the middle of the night."

Sybil got out her pad. Apparently, she had not heard about the latest problem. "A masked figure you say, Mrs. Bishop?"

"Oh, call me Lucinda. Everybody does."

Maggie sat bolt upright. The two women were startled.

"Anyone want a sandwich? Mom packed a delicious lunch."

"Now be back here at three o'clock sharp," Mr. Porter told Christie & Company as he rowed them in to the town wharf. He'd already made one trip in the dinghy with the Bishops and Sybil Corcoran. "I'm meeting the Howes to pick up a special order of that focaccia and the jalapeño cheese bread they make for your mother; then I'll be back here."

Maggie nodded. She hoped Mary Howe would slip in some of her sticky buns, as she'd done in the past. Penobscot Bay Provisions was a bakery and specialty food shop in Stonington. Her mother had found soul mates in Rich and Mary, relying on them to stock her freezer with some of the things she didn't have time to bake.

"Okay," Maggie replied, "that gives us almost two hours. We won't be late." She hoped the other passengers were on time. She was willing to bet Sybil would be. Main Street, Stonington wasn't exactly Madison Avenue, and the city sophisticate would probably get bored quickly.

Maggie was wrong. The first place the girls went was the Eastern Bay Craft Gallery. Sybil was already there, and from the look of it she was going to need the dinghy all to herself for the return trip to the sailboat.

"Aren't these jackets heavenly!" she called out to them, holding one up. It was hand-woven and the price was celestial, too.

"Must be nice to be rich," Maggie whispered to her friends, "and I doubt I'm ever going to find out." They laughed and browsed. Christie bought a tiny pillow covered with patchwork and filled with balsam pine needles. When she wanted to remember Little Bittern, the scent would bring it all back.

"Let's go across the street to that place we passed

and get some ice cream," Vicky suggested. "For some reason, I'm starving."

"It's the salt air," Maggie said. "Although, I can always eat the Austins' ice cream. Plus, they have a deck where we can sit and see the whole harbor."

They said good-bye to Sybil Corcoran, who was definitely enjoying herself now that she was able to exercise her talents as a shopper. Maggie hoped it would blot out the nasty comments Mrs. Bishop had made about the inn on the trip over.

She told the other two about the conversation while they were licking their cones, gazing out across the water to the islands in the distance—pincushions of uneven pines scattered along the horizon.

"People like that always want to make themselves seem more important than they are," Vicky said emphatically.

"True, but when you think of Mr. Bishop's conversation with Hap, it seems as if both of them want to make the Porters look bad." Christie let the chocolate ice cream melt on her tongue. Maggie was right. She could eat this anytime.

Maggie shook her head. "It's like a puzzle you buy at a yard sale. You're almost finished and then there are pieces missing. Why would the Bishops want to make the inn look bad?"

No one had a plausible answer. Vicky was just about to ask a question when Christie poked her in the arm. "Look," she whispered.

It was the woman from the ferry. Today her auburn hair wasn't pulled back under a scarf and it glistened richly in the sunlight. She'd bought a sandwich and a milk shake and was sitting at the next table.

"So, she wasn't staying on Little Bittern," Maggie said softly.

"I have a feeling she is," Christie said slowly. In her mind, she saw the tinted photo she'd just discovered in their cottage and the portrait of the joyous child in the meadow hanging on a wall as clearly as if both were before her now.

"Well," Maggie said, jumping up, "let's go. I want to show you the rest of the town. We didn't stop to look at the miniature houses, remember."

They had passed the little village, complete with Clam Flat Elementary School, church, and stores, on their way to the gallery. The original houses had been located on the lawn of the man who made them as a hobby; then when someone else bought the house, a permanent home was found on Main Street.

"Why don't I meet you there? I'd like to finish my cone and look at the view a little longer," Christie said.

Vicky gave her a questioning look but said, "No problem," then pulled Maggie away. "We'll walk slowly."

"Thanks," Christie said.

She wasn't sure how she was going to start a conversation, yet she knew she had to try. She might not get another chance.

In the end, she simply walked over to the woman, sat down across from her, and said, "You're Mrs. Griffith's daughter, aren't you?"

❖Chapter Seven

"**W**HY, YES. YES, I AM." THE WOMAN PUT her sandwich down and looked at Christie intently. "You were on the ferry with another girl. I remember you." Her voice was rich, transforming the simple statement into something more dramatic. She must be an actress, Christie thought.

"But," continued the woman, "how did you know that, and who are *you?*"

Christie seemed to be introducing herself to the Griffiths with some frequency. "My name is Christie Montgomery and I'm visiting the Porters, who own the Blue Heron Inn."

"Oh, the inn." Again, the way she spoke invested the words with subtle meaning—a darker meaning.

"Your mother lets me use the pool. I'm a diver. But it's a secret. I mean, she said if I told anyone, I couldn't use it."

"Yet you've told me." The woman smiled the way the leader does when saying, "I didn't say Simon says" after someone moves.

Christie felt herself getting flushed. "I thought you might have come to see her. And in a way, it's your pool, too." What she left unsaid was, So it isn't like telling an outsider.

"At one time, it was my pool completely. She put it in for me. Some notion of swimming glory—the Olympics, the English Channel. Oh, it was so long ago." The woman laughed. Christie thought she had never seen a more animated face—it was younger, prettier when she was talking.

They both paused, and Christie realized she hadn't answered the first question. "I recognized you from the pictures—both pictures. Except one is of your mother, I think. A photograph. She's wearing a green dress with a fancy lace collar."

"That was her graduation picture. I haven't seen it for many years. Where is it?"

"I'm afraid it's just stacked against a wall in one of the cottages at the inn. There are a lot of photographs and prints stored there. Why didn't your family take them when they left?"

"You haven't heard the story?"

"No. What story?" Christie asked eagerly.

The woman seemed to be making up her mind. "You haven't said what the other picture is."

"It's a painting—in your mother's living room. A little girl is running through a field of daisies." As she described it, Christie could hear Mrs. Griffith's words: "I *had* a child."

"That is of me. I was seven years old and thought the world would always be full of fields of daisies."

Suddenly, Christie felt she couldn't keep the thought that had been pushing its way to the front of her mind bottled up any longer. "My mother's dead. She died a year and a half ago. You *have* a mother. Why can't you go to the house and see her? You were looking for her on the dock, weren't you? You came to the island, so you must want to see her."

"It's not so simple, mothers and daughters. Or maybe it is when put in your terms. I'm sorry about your mother, only you see, little Christie, I may want to see mine, but she doesn't want to see me."

Christie felt like a balloon the day after a party, slowly deflating. She could imagine Mrs. Griffith holding whatever grudge she had against her daughter. She could imagine it very well.

"I have tried to see her," the woman continued, "but she won't even talk to me on the phone."

"But what happened? Why is she so angry with you?"

The light disappeared from the lovely face before Christie and the woman suddenly looked old. "I made a decision she didn't agree with. She said I'd be destroying my life, her life.

"Grandfather and Grandmother had died. Griffith's Nest—that's what the house, now the inn, was always called—had been rented for the summer. Friends came to visit the tenants. A theatrical family, a family with a son." Caroline Griffith's daughter looked out across the harbor at the islands interrupting the horizon. She seemed to forget Christie was there. "He was so golden—golden hair, shining skin—and lucky. Already on Broadway. Together, we were going to be a golden couple. The renters' teenaged son was taking us to the mainland in his sailboat. We were of age and didn't need our parents' consent. I made the mistake of telling my mother. I wanted her blessing. I got her curse. And it worked. The boat capsized. I was the only survivor."

Christie reached for her hand. "Can't you simply appear? Go to the house—I'm sure she won't turn you away. All these years . . . And it was an accident! She didn't make it happen. Neither did you."

She ignored Christie's plea.

"Griffith's Nest was closed up. Mother put the whole thing in trust for a charity. No Griffiths ever went in it again. And I'm afraid you would have a very hard time convincing my mother that the place wasn't cursed. It was where she met my father, too."

Cursed! The Blue Heron Inn? What had the Porters gotten themselves into?

Just as Christie was going to try to convince Caroline's daughter further, Maggie and Vicky came around the corner of the building.

"Christie, we have to go! Dad will be furious if we keep everybody waiting." Maggie stopped short when she saw who was sitting with her friend.

"I'm sorry." Christie jumped up. "I lost track of the time. These are my friends, Maggie Porter and Vicky Lee. This is . . ." She realized she didn't know the daughter's name.

"Diane Griffith. You best hurry—and tell your father it was all my fault." She smiled at Maggie, then turned to Christie. "Thanks for the advice. You're a very wise child. And telling me doesn't count. After all, it was mine once."

Christie nodded, knowing she meant the pool, but the other two girls were looking very puzzled.

"You can tell us all about it on the way back," Maggie said softly but firmly.

"Good-bye. I hope I'll see you again," Christie called to Diane as she followed her friends.

"Good-bye. I hope so, too."

But neither of them knew when or how that would ever be.

The sail back was as beautiful as the trip over. The entire boat was lulled into silence by the feeling of the end of the day, the voyage home. The sharp cries of the laughing gulls provided most of the conversation, except for the small group at the bow, where Christie was telling her friends as much as she could. She was feeling stubborn. She didn't want to give up the pool, so she couldn't reveal that she had met Mrs. Griffith. She let them think she and Diane had drifted into conversation there on the Austins' deck. The fact that it was an unusually intimate one was not lost on the other two, who both eyed her at the end of the tale. Vicky gave voice to their thoughts.

"Strange that she would say all this to you."

Christie didn't respond. She was feeling guilty enough and didn't want to lie.

"I know that voice," Vicky added, "but not the face." Vicky was an active member of the Drama Club, well versed in stage and screen personalities.

Maggie was slightly stunned by the inn's history— a history she was sure her parents didn't know. It explained a lot. Why it was so hard to get help, for instance. Obviously, everyone on the island knew about Griffith's Nest and its dark past—everyone but the Porters. It was one thing to buy a haunted inn. They'd looked at some of those. Guests liked the idea of a friendly ghost or two. But tragedy and a family divided—that was different. For once, the daydream she tumbled into wasn't about herself.

The two lovers ran to meet each other on the shore. Her hair was loose, tossed by the wind. "Hurry, my darling," he said. "The wind is starting to pick up. We can just make it across." They met in an embrace.

"Come on," the boy shouted. "Time enough for that later." He was excited. For a week, he'd carried their notes back and forth; now he'd carry them. They pushed off and the sail snapped, then pulled taut. The small skiff flew across the water. His cheeks were red, eyes glistening.

"We'll name our first son after you," the man called out.

Then it happened. So quickly. The cold water. The overturned boat. "Hold on," she screamed to them. "Don't let go. Hold on!"

"What do you think we should do?"

Maggie said, "Do?"

"I mean should we tell your parents or what?" Vicky asked.

"I don't know," Maggie said slowly. "They have so much on their minds right now. It may not be the best moment for them to find out about Griffith's Nest and its secret. I think I should ask George."

"An excellent plan," Christie agreed.

"And Malvina. She's very sensible. Plus, there's something else I want to talk to her about."

Neither Christie nor Vicky asked what that was, but both remembered that Malvina was Charlene's grandmother. Maggie's friend Charlene, who wouldn't even return her phone calls these days.

"You don't think that the things going on at the inn now have any connection with what happened before?" Christie asked, filled with a sense of foreboding.

"How could they be?" Vicky was emphatic. "No, the stuff that's happening is definitely in the here and now."

Just how here and now was waiting for them when they got back to the Blue Heron. Visibly upset, Mrs. Porter dragged her husband into the kitchen. She didn't appear to notice the three curious girls who followed.

"A snake in the bed in room fifteen. Fortunately, Malvina found it before the guests did. Only a garter snake, but you remember the woman went on and on the other night about how terrified she was of *any* kind of snake. Then there's vinegar in the cream I was planning to use for tonight's crème brûlée. I can't stand much more of this! What are we going to do! You know how fast word gets around! We could go out of business!"

"Honey, sit down. You know those snakes get in from time to time. It's just coincidence, and what makes you so sure there's vinegar in the cream? Maybe it's a bad lot? We can't let this all get blown out of proportion. It's silly even to think of closing." Ned Porter sounded calm and rational. His wife took a deep breath.

"Maybe you're right. It's just that I've had such an odd feeling all day."

"Of course you have. It was very upsetting having the Logans leave and influencing those others to go early. Now, let us help get the hors d'oeuvres ready for cocktails. That will leave you time to take a good soak in a nice warm bath."

Maggie's mother managed a wobbly smile. "Oh, you think that's the cure for everything."

"Well, isn't it?"

Christie & Company looked at one another.

Not this time, Dad, Maggie mouthed.

Malvina Compton was still in the laundry room, ironing. She was working Sunday so she could take the Fourth off. Maggie hoisted herself up on one of the washers. It wasn't unusual for her to sit and chat with Malvina, but for once, she felt awkward.

"Cat got your tongue?" Malvina asked. "Never knew you to be at a loss for words."

Maggie had intended to talk to her about the inn, but instead she said, "Do you know why Charlene is mad at me? Why she won't talk to me anymore?" The last words came out slightly choked. Maggie was close to tears.

Malvina stopped ironing and stood next to Maggie. Over the years, Maggie and Willy had become almost as important to her as her own grandchildren. She put her hand on Maggie's shoulder.

"Now, you're a smart girl and I've known you a long time. Think a minute and you'll figure it out, startin' with the question, What's different about this summer from last?"

Maggie sat up straighter and sniffed. She didn't have a tissue. Malvina did, and she handed it to Maggie.

"Well, last summer, Charlene wasn't working. We were together every day. It was great."

Malvina nodded encouragingly. "Go on."

"This summer, I hardly see her, and my friends from school are here, too." The moment she said the words out loud, she knew that was it.

"How could I have been so stupid! But I thought we were better friends than that. How could Charlene think I wouldn't be her friend anymore because Christie and Vicky are here?"

"Could be she thinks a year at that fancy school has changed you from what you used to be. And those two girls from away don't look like they're getting their duds at Wal-Mart."

"But I haven't changed. I'm still the same!"

"You may know that and I may know that, but does Charlene?"

Maggie shook her head. "There hasn't been any time for us to be together."

"Mondays are her day off. Sundays, too."

"It's too late to do anything today." As she said this, Maggie realized she hadn't even thought to include Charlene in the sail, when of course the Co-Op was closed on Sundays. Maybe she hadn't been such a good friend after all. Last summer, she and Charlene had often gone out in the boat when there was space.

"But we'll all do something tomorrow. She'll see Christie and Vicky aren't snobby rich girls, or whatever it is she thinks. Vicky gets all those clothes at Filene's Basement and thrift stores."

Malvina was still looking at her. Maggie knew she hadn't gotten it right yet.

"Maybe I should do something just with Charlene, then later all of us together."

Malvina gave her a hug. "There now, deah, I knew you were smart."

Maggie was about to leave when she remembered the other reason she'd come. She told Malvina about Christie's talk with Diane Griffith.

"She was the most beautiful girl ever to live on this island. She was raised here, you know. Caroline wouldn't let her go away to school. She went along with everybody else, then had some special tutors who came when she was older. Caroline couldn't bear for that child to be out of her sight for a moment. It wasn't right. We all knew it, but you could never tell the Griffiths anything. They were that stubborn. Caroline herself went against her parents to marry, and even when it went all to pieces, she still wouldn't admit she'd been wrong. 'I got Diane, didn't I?' she'd say. Well, it did turn out tragic. Diane eloping and the others in the boat drowned—one only a boy. Well, you heard the story. This house was closed up until your parents bought it."

"But do people on the island think it's cursed somehow?"

"I wouldn't go that far. But maybe there's a few who think it's a bit unlucky. I don't hold with superstition, although"—Malvina laughed—"that first summer here to the inn I was having my doubts, especially when Willy gave half the population chicken pox!"

"But you don't think so now," Maggie insisted.

"No, I don't," Malvina declared. "Whatever shenanigans are happening are just that."

"Do you think I should tell my parents about the Griffiths?"

Malvina Compton had resumed her ironing. She brushed a wisp of hair from her hot forehead. "That's a hard one. Ordinarily, I'd say yes, but why don't you wait a day or two? Let these other things blow over. The Blue Heron is a lovely place, and your parents have made it what it is. We don't want anything to spoil that," she said firmly.

Maggie gave her a big hug. "That's what I think, too, and now I've got to call Charlene."

The door slammed behind her. Malvina shook her head. "Hope I'm right," she said under her breath.

After breakfast the next morning, Maggie took her bike to Charlene's house. The night before, she'd come right to the point on the phone, and now both girls couldn't wait to see each other. Charlene *had* been jealous of Vicky and Christie. "They're so perfect, Mags!" Charlene had said. Maggie hadn't really thought about it, but it was true that stylish Vicky with her beautiful long hair and a smile that made everyone else want to smile, too, and Christie with her shiny cap of blond hair and lithe athletic body would have made Maggie herself jealous if the tables were turned and they were Charlene's friends.

Vicky was teaching Mrs. Porter to make pot stickers and Christie announced she was going to take a walk.

"You seem to have fallen in love with the shore,"

Mrs. Porter said. "The tide is out. If you walk to the right of the inn, facing the water, you'll see some magnificent tide pools."

Since that was the way Christie had planned to go, she was quick to agree.

"Maggie is bringing Charlene back here and we'll pack a lunch for you all," Mrs. Porter continued. "You have a watch, don't you?"

"Yes, Christie," Vicky said slyly. "You know how you lost track of time yesterday."

Christie would have stuck out her tongue if Mrs. Porter hadn't been there. She knew her friends believed she was keeping something from them—and she was. But not for long, she hoped.

She went straight to the pool after doing her stretches. An hour later, she towel-dried her hair and changed into dry clothes, stuffing her things into the small backpack she'd carried. Then she went up to the back door of the house and knocked. Marie answered.

"I wonder if I could see Mrs. Griffith for a moment?" Christie asked.

Marie closed the door in her face, and Christie could only presume she was going to make the request.

The door opened and Marie said curtly, "Follow me."

Mrs. Griffith was upstairs, sitting in a large chair by the window. From this view, you could see as far as Mount Desert Island.

"Sit down, sit down. Pool too cold? Want me to have the temperature turned up?"

Christie waited until she heard Marie shut the door.

"No, it's fine. I'm just not sure I'll be able to use it anymore. I told someone."

A triumphant look crossed the old woman's face. "Didn't think you could keep a secret."

"I told your daughter. Your daughter, Diane."

"Diane," Mrs. Griffith whispered. Then she stood up. "I think you'd better be on your way. I told you, I don't have a child."

"But you do. She's so beautiful and her voice—her voice is like . . . well, it makes you imagine you can read her mind, everything she's feeling."

Mrs. Griffith was listening carefully. She sat down.

"I saw her first on the ferry. We all noticed her hair."

"Long, is it still long?"

Christie nodded. "Then I saw a photograph in storage at the inn. It was her face and hair, but the picture was an old one. It was also *your* face. I could tell. You were wearing a green dress."

"I loved that dress. It was silk and the lace came from France. It's still in a trunk in the attic."

"And the child in the painting downstairs has the same red hair. After I saw the photo, I knew she was your child."

"Quite the little detective, aren't you. Well, Nancy Drew, or whoever you are, I repeat, go back to the inn and swim in the ocean. Dive from the rocks. I don't want to see you—or her—again," Caroline Griffith said, resuming her acerbic tone.

Christie stood up and faced Mrs. Griffith, blocking

the old lady's precious view of the water. A view—
that was all Mrs. Griffith had. Christie felt an anger
begin to build up inside her—an anger so intense,
it frightened her, before it took over completely and
spilled out.

"But *she* wants to see you!" Christie shouted.
"Doesn't that matter to you at all! Diane's your
daughter, the only daughter you'll ever have. She's
been here before, hasn't she? And each time, you've
turned her away!" Christie had to hold her arms rig-
idly at her sides to keep herself from shaking the
woman in front of her. She realized her fists were
clenched. Mrs. Griffith's mouth had dropped open in
surprise, but she didn't say anything. Christie's
rage increased.

"I don't care if I ever see you again or swim in your
stupid pool. Making me keep the secret was cruel,
but nothing like what you're doing to Diane. You're
just throwing a daughter away. I know that no matter what I'd done or how much I'd hurt her, *my*
mother would never have treated me this way!"

Christie started to cry. "You don't deserve her,
you . . ." The emotion was too strong. She felt almost
sick now. Trembling, she stumbled to the door. She
put her hand on the knob and pulled it open. But
before she left, she stopped and, controlling her voice,
said in harsh, steady tones, "You wanted to know
what they were saying on the island about you. They
say you're a witch! And they're right!"

She ran down the stairs and out the front door.
There were stairs to the beach here, too. Partly

blinded by her tears, she found her way down, collapsing on the rocky beach at the bottom, sobbing.

"It isn't fair," she cried aloud to the seabirds. "Why is *she* alive and Mom gone?"

If the other girls noticed that Christie seemed a bit down, nobody said anything. Maggie had told Charlene about Molly Montgomery's death. Vicky and Maggie had also talked to a counselor at school about how they could best help their friend with her grief, and she'd advised them to be sensitive to Christie's moods. "Don't always try to cheer her up. Let her talk about her mother. Create opportunities. But if her sadness goes on for too long or it seems at all desperate, let me or another adult know immediately."

"Willy's got a stockpile of Roman candles and all sorts of firecrackers. He's planning a noisy Fourth of July," Maggie said. They were sitting in the woods on a high rock. The trees around them were draped with moss and they were enjoying the slightly eerie feeling. What a great place for ghost stories, Vicky had said when Maggie and Charlene had led them to this, one of their favorite spots.

"I love the Fourth of July," Vicky said. "Will there be fireworks?"

Charlene answered, "Oh, there'll be fireworks! Plenty of them!"

And she was right.

Chapter Eight

THE FOURTH OF JULY DAWNED HAZY, HOT, and humid. Almost like summer in the city, Christie thought.

For once, Vicky had slept in and she grumbled about having to take such a short shower. The girls passed Darnell Sanford on their way into the kitchen.

"See you all down at the harbor later? It looks like a storm's on the way. Feel how still it is? Just hope it holds off until after the fireworks," he called out to them.

"Everyone's going down to Green Harbor after breakfast to spend the day. Then tonight we're having lobster on the beach for the guests. It can't rain!" Maggie answered. She didn't want anything to go wrong today. Sybil Corcoran was in a good mood after the outing to Stonington and had told the Porters how much she was looking forward to an "old-fashioned Down East Fourth of July." The Blue Heron was doing everything in its power to supply one, from the morning's blueberry pancakes to the evening's red lobster.

After a quick breakfast, the girls rode their bikes

to town. They'd promised to help Charlene and the others get ready for the Fish and Fritter Fry sponsored by the Fishermen's Wives Association for their scholarship fund. The parade would start at ten, followed by games for children at the schoolhouse. The Fry started at one o'clock and went on all afternoon.

"When I was younger, I used to decorate my bike with streamers and ride in the parade. All the kids did. Willy and his friends still do. We'll have to clap extra hard for them," Maggie told her friends. She kind of missed those days.

"Wow, look at the decorations!" Vicky exclaimed as they came down the steep hill into Green Harbor. There were flags, streamers, and bunting everywhere. People had already started to gather for the parade, and a feeling of anticipation filled the air.

"Maggie! Over here!" It was George. He was taking the day off, he'd told them. "I saved some places!"

The girls parked their bikes and walked over to where George had staked out a prime location right beside the judges' viewing stand, normally the front porch of the town hall.

"Can you save them a little longer?" Maggie asked. "We have to check in with Charlene."

"Okay, but don't be too long," George answered.

The Fish and Fritter Fry was held at the ferry landing. Charlene, her mother, and other island women were setting up long tables. This year, they'd added chowder to the menu, and the big pots were sending forth delicious smells. Charlene's mother reassured them they wouldn't be needed until after the games, so all four girls went to watch the parade.

"Look." Christie laughed. "I think the St. Clairs and their friends got their dates wrong. They must think this is the U.S. Open Tennis Match or something."

All of them were in the whitest of tennis whites, complete with wristbands and visors.

"What's their racket?" Vicky quipped.

"They probably plan to play after the parade. There are some courts and a golf course at the Little Bittern Country Club, but nobody gets all decked up like that," Maggie said.

"A country club? On the island?" Christie was surprised.

"It was started by some islanders and summer people a long time ago. Everybody uses it. I guess I never thought much about the name, but it is funny. We have a one-room schoolhouse *and* a country club."

"Does it have a pool?" Christie asked anxiously. She knew there would be no more diving practice at Mrs. Griffith's after what had happened the day before.

"Sorry—and we haven't done the swimming I promised. So much seems to be happening," Maggie said apologetically.

"Don't worry," Christie replied. "Look, they're starting."

The parade was a labor of love. This year, the theme was Maine products, and the islanders had used great ingenuity to construct their floats.

George was laughing. "That's my Uncle Elwell's. He's been working on it for months. Thought my aunt was going to leave him for spending so much time in the barn."

The result was *something,* though—a giant lobster trap, complete with papier-mâché lobsters. It was all mounted on the back of his pickup, which was covered by crumbled-up wads of watery blue paper. A huge lobster pot, painted with the Stars and Stripes, was attached to the top of the truck's cab.

The truck was followed by a dozen of the youngest residents of Little Bittern, whose mothers had slaved away making roly-poly blueberry costumes. "They're so cute!" Vicky cried, "I like that kid over there with the blueberry juice on her chin. It looks so real."

"It is!" the child shouted as she marched proudly by, reaching inside her costume for some more of the berries she'd tucked away.

After the parade, which went through the small village twice, they all went up to the school, where Maggie and George won the water-balloon toss for kids over twelve and Vicky won the sack race for their age group, much to her surprise.

Sporting their ribbons, they returned to the landing. It was almost noon. Hap Hotchkiss was walking about in the growing crowd, carrying a clipboard and buttonholing people.

"What's he up to?" Maggie asked. She didn't trust him.

George frowned. "He's trying to get people to sign a petition he's sending to Augusta. Seems the state has turned down his plans for Isle-Away. He's appealing the decision and wants everyone to support him. Says how good the development will be for the island's economy."

"But that's nonsense!" Maggie was passionate about the subject. "My parents say his plans will destroy a unique part of Little Bittern and not provide much in the way of jobs after the initial construction, and he'll probably bring off-islanders to do it, anyway. The land he bought is a nesting ground for many seabirds. Too bad he didn't do his homework."

George agreed with Maggie. "I don't like the guy. Nobody does. He's the kind who comes around flashing all his money, but he doesn't care any more about us than . . . well, than we do about him and his time-sharing, whatever that is."

"Why did the people sell the land in the first place if it was so special?" Vicky asked.

"Because they needed the money," George answered bluntly. "It was owned by the Harpers—it's called Harper Point. Neville's last stay at Maine Medical just about bankrupted them."

"Maybe if Hap can't develop it, they'll be able to buy it back somehow, like damaged goods," Christie suggested optimistically.

George shook his head. He knew better. "It does seem that Hap's sniffing around, though. Came to my dad, told him to name his price for the cove. Dad told him it would cost him a dollar for every grain of sand. Hap was pretty steamed."

As they walked by the man, who was wearing a bright blue blazer and red-striped shirt for the occasion, they could see he didn't have too many names on his petition. He was beginning to look slightly steamed again.

Maggie tried to see who had signed, but the angle was wrong. She was surprised that Hap had tried to buy Sanford Cove. She wouldn't have thought he'd give up so easily, and although the cove was beautiful, there wasn't as much land as there was at Harper Point. "Isle-Away." She wished he would simply go away.

Charlene and Maggie were soon hard at work frying clam fritters. Vicky and Christie kept them supplied with plates. Willy came by with some of his friends. A moment later, everyone jumped as a string of firecrackers went off next to the table. The boys scooted away.

"William Porter!" Maggie fumed. "That was not funny! I'm going to kill you!"

"Hey, Mags, I used to do the same thing at his age. In fact, I've got a few in my pocket now. Don't be so hard on Willy," George said, coming back for his third helping.

"I know, but he's not just immature; he's terminally immature—and they shouldn't be setting them off in the middle of a crowd. You never did that."

By the end of the afternoon, two things were clear: The Fishermen's Wives Association had broken its record for number of potatoes peeled, onions chopped, clams shucked, fish cleaned, and a storm was on its way. It was still hot and the air felt heavy. All day, the sky had been gray and cloudy.

"No fireworks tonight—and maybe no lobster on the beach," Maggie told her friends in a resigned tone. "They'll save the fireworks for the first clear Saturday night, so you might get to see them yet. Now, we'd better get back and see what's going on at the inn." Silently, she hoped that nothing was. All the guests had been at the festivities with her father and seemed to be having a good time. She'd been startled to see Sybil Corcoran with a huge cone of cotton candy that she was delicately consuming, pulling tiny pieces from it with the tips of two fingers. Her nephew was at her side—or a bit to the rear, actually. He had grease on his shirt from his fritters, and soon disappeared into the crowd—banned, no doubt, by his aunt for untidiness.

"What do you think? Should we take a chance?" Mrs. Porter was uncharacteristically hesitant. "I'm sure if we lug everything down, it will begin to pour. If we don't, the weather will clear."

"Why don't you have your cocktail hour on the beach, then serve the rest of the dinner on the porch? People can always duck inside if it starts to rain, but this way, if it doesn't, it will still be outdoors," Vicky suggested. She and Mrs. Porter had made Maine pot stickers, stuffing the crescents of dough with a mixture of crab, scallions, and spices. It would be easy enough to eat them on the beach, along with the other tidbits Mrs. Porter had prepared.

"Perfect. Now let's get busy!" Julia Porter seemed like her old self, and Maggie shot her friend a grateful look. She might have her differences with her superefficient, always-right mom, yet she didn't want her to change—at least not at the moment.

Down at the shore, the Porters contentedly surveyed the munching crowd of guests exclaiming over the view, a dramatic sky filled with darkening storm clouds.

Christie & Company were sitting on a rock, nibbling from a plate of goodies. They were chatting away about the day's events.

"It's the best Fourth of July I've ever spent," Christie said. Vicky vigorously nodded agreement. Her mouth was full.

"And it's not over yet." Maggie was glad her friends had enjoyed Little Bittern's festivities. She would long remember how Vicky's face looked after the blueberry pie–eating contest. "I've got some sparklers we can light when it gets dark enough."

"The great lady's nephew is giving a very realistic 'suffering artist' performance," Vicky said, lowering her voice. "Look at him over there by himself. Maybe he has writer's block. He certainly seems to be in pain."

"More likely too many clam fritters. He kept coming back for more. Malvina said she thought he must have two stomachs," Christie added.

The girls giggled. Paul Corcoran did present a picture of woe, slightly slumped over a plate of food he wasn't touching.

"I made the mistake of asking him how his writing was going and he almost took my head off," Maggie told them. "I guess it was dumb of me. Writers are supposed to be supersensitive about where they are in their work."

"But he could have been nicer," Christie pointed

out. "He seems so pathetic. I feel sorry for the guy. Having a famous relative in sort of the same business must be hard. Admit it, Sybil's a tough act to follow."

"He's certainly trying. That ancient typewriter of his clickety-clacks from morning to night. I heard it when I passed his cabin this afternoon after we got back. I hope I'll have half the discipline he does." Maggie's dream was to be an author.

"Probably most of it lands in the wastebasket," Vicky said cynically. "He just doesn't seem like somebody with a great book in him."

"And how can you tell, Miss Literary Authority?" Maggie asked somewhat anxiously. Had Vicky already come to some conclusion about her?

"His face is too boring. He doesn't look as if he's really lived." She exaggerated the last words, mocking her own romanticism. Secretly, Maggie agreed with her, but she admired any writer as diligent as Paul.

"She's been in her study for weeks! And scarcely a bite to eat." Her two friends stood uncertainly outside Margaret Porter's door.

"You know how she gets when inspiration hits, and after the last book, there's so much pressure on her to come up with another best-seller."

The other woman nodded. "True. How many authors are translated into every language in the world and have the movie adaptation win ten Oscars!"

Suddenly, the door was opened wide.

"It's finished! I'm calling it For the Love Of."

"For the love of what, or whom?"

"You'll have to read the book to find out." A brilliant title, a brilliant book, she hoped. She was exhausted. She rang for some champagne. Who better to celebrate with than her best friends? For the love of . . .

Mrs. Porter walked over to them.

"Maggie, have you seen Willy since you got back from town?"

"No. The last I saw of him was at the Fry, around three o'clock." She was tempted to squeal on her brother, but George was right. The firecrackers were no big deal. Still, she'd let Willy have a piece of her mind.

"He was supposed to come straight home afterward. He must be up at the house."

"I bet he's practicing the knots George taught him," Vicky said, giving Maggie a knowing look. She'd made her friend blush deep red with her theory about why George was having Willy practice so diligently— a theory that involved spending time with Maggie without her little brother around!

Christie had tuned out of the conversation. All day, she'd searched the crowd for Diane Griffith—or her mother. She did see Marie and her husband. They got on the ferry for the mainland. Mrs. Griffith must have given them the holiday off. At least she wasn't that mean. Christie hoped the absence of both Griffiths meant that they were together. It was so complicated, but also so easy. They just had to get over the first wall—the wall they'd erected together.

The Bishops strolled over.

"These little crab things are scrumptious, Julia.

You must give me the recipe so I can try them! I've been eating like a pig today—that yummy fish fry," Lucinda gushed.

Maggie and her mother exchanged glances. It was a private joke between them. The Bishops had a cook, yet Lucinda was always asking for recipes, which Mrs. Porter would give her. The fact was, the woman could scarcely boil water, let alone whip up some crab pot stickers. And Bobbie was even worse. She had once called the Porters when they were all living in the same building to ask how to turn on the oven. She was home alone and wanted to warm a pizza. At present, she and her hubby, Chad, were perched on a rock far away from the rest of the guests. They'd grabbed their drinks and some food and left, making it clear that there was no one interesting enough for them. Sybil Corcoran had watched the young couple leave, and Maggie thought she heard the woman say, "Dime a dozen," but the words were muffled by the large flag-motif scarf Sybil had wound around her neck.

"Everybody's here," Vicky said suddenly.

Christie rejoined the conversation. "What do you mean?"

"I mean all the suspects—even Hap."

Maggie nodded. There were several additions to the inn guests for dinner, and Hap was one, at least for cocktails. Afterward, he was taking the Bishops to the house he'd rented. They were going to have their own private lobster feast. Julia Porter had been extremely annoyed when Lucinda had told her—only an hour ago.

Back at the inn, there was still no sign of Willy, but everyone was too busy boiling lobsters and corn to do more than make a passing remark about him. Maggie's was slightly gloating: "Boy, is he in trouble!" Ned Porter's was firm: "I don't like Willy's leaving again with his friends and not telling us where. Malvina said she heard a bunch of firecrackers go off earlier, so he must have been here. He needs to be reminded about his responsibilities."

Maggie's mother was carrying a basket of buttermilk biscuits out to the porch. So far, the rain had held off. "I know. He's only ten, not a teenager yet."

Willy had still not shown up by dessert. Julia had prepared a variety of favorites—apple and blueberry pies, devil's food cake, brownies, fresh strawberries, and mounds of vanilla ice cream or whipped cream to go on top of everything.

"Ned, why don't you call George and see if Willy's there? And if not, try some of his other friends."

Ned came back immediately. "The phone's out. Someone must have hit a pole, or maybe the storm's already started on the other side of the island. I'm going to take the car and go over to the Sanfords'."

Again, he was back right away, this time his face ashen. He didn't seem to be aware of the guests or anyone else. He looked squarely at his wife.

"Those weren't firecrackers Malvina heard. Someone's shot holes in the tires of all the cars."

A woman screamed. It was Bobbie St. Clair.

"Willy!" cried Julia Porter. "Where *is* he!"

Just then, George and Darnell Sanford came up the drive. Rain was beginning to fall in big drops—

hard, like lead. Abandoning the food, for which no one had any taste now, people crowded into the inn's living room. Darnell motioned the Porters to one side of the porch before they could go in. The girls quickly ran over.

"Is everything okay here?" Darnell asked.

Ned spoke rapidly. "Some idiot, or worse, has used all the car tires for target practice, and it's shaken us up."

George looked startled. Darnell spoke slowly. "I was afraid of something like this. My hunting rifle's missing."

Maggie grabbed his arm, "Willy's missing, too!"

❖Chapter Nine

"**A**RE YOU SURE?" GEORGE ASKED. "WHEN I left the harbor, he told me he was going straight home, and that was about four o'clock. Maybe he fell asleep in the barn. You know he's got that hiding place there."

The Porters didn't know.

"What hiding place?" Ned asked.

"In the hayloft. He put an old armchair and one of those battery-powered lanterns up there. He takes his comics. Lately, he's been practicing his knots."

Ned and Julia were already off the porch, running in the direction of the barn. Everyone else followed. A brilliant flash of lightning heralded a loud clap of thunder. Vicky thought if Willy had nodded off, he must surely be awake now.

But the loft was empty. There was no sign of Willy anywhere in the barn. No sign until Maggie spied a red crepe-paper streamer sticking out from under an old tarp. She pulled it off.

Beneath the cover was Willy's bike.

"We have to get through to the State Police and

the Coast Guard! I'm going to start searching the woods," Julia Porter said, frantic.

Darnell Sanford took her arm. "Best thing for you, deah, is to stay at the inn to welcome him home. And the phone may come back at any moment. You know how that happens. I'll get ahold of the police and Coast Guard on my CB and call around the island. Meanwhile, George and Ned can start looking for Willy. He may have seen the storm coming and ducked out of the way someplace. I'd try the boat-house first. Maggie, you go with your mother now."

Seeing Willy's bike with its proud decorations was almost more than Maggie could bear. Her brain screamed the last words she'd said to her brother: "I'm going to kill you!" But Darnell's calm, take-charge attitude had its effect, and she tried to concentrate on his words: "Welcome him home." As they left the barn, Maggie's mother's arm clutching her daughter's shoulder, Mrs. Porter stopped and turned to face her husband. "This is it, Ned. The Blue Heron goes up for sale tomorrow." Bleakly, he nodded his head in agreement.

In the living room, the guests were huddled in small, frightened groups. Vicky announced she was making coffee and was rewarded by a few appreciative glances. As she went toward the kitchen, she asked Maggie, who was sitting close to her mother on the couch, "If the phone is out, does that mean the lights will go out, too?"

"More than likely. In fact, I'm surprised they're still on."

Outside, the storm was pelting the windows with

rain so hard, it seemed the glass would shatter at any moment. Thunder crashed and the lightning seemed only a few feet away.

"I'm scared," whimpered Bobbie St. Clair, and reached for her husband's hand. "This place will go up like a matchbox if we get hit by lightning."

Panic appeared on several faces. "There are plenty of lightning rods. Please don't worry," Mrs. Porter said in a dull voice, then added, "Maggie, get the lamps and candles in case we do lose power."

Christie went with Vicky into the kitchen and started the coffee. The stove was gas and they made it on that, not wanting to chance the electric cof- feemaker. Soon, the reassuring smell filled the air and the girls distributed brimming mugs. A few of the guests took some of the dessert, hastily pulled from the porch, which was now drenched with water.

Then they waited.

The first thing that happened was that the lights did go out. Again, a woman screamed. Again, it was Bobbie. Maggie scurried around lighting candles and lamps. The room slowly came to life. As she passed by Sybil Corcoran, she heard the woman comment to the person next to her, "I'm afraid this does it for my story. The moment I can get out of here, I will."

"Me, too" was the unfortunate reply.

Let them leave, Maggie thought angrily. The sooner the better. Let them all leave. Just please let us find Willy safe and sound. She repeated this over and over as she sat with the others in the semidarkness.

After awhile, she got up and went over first to

Vicky, then to Christie, whispering the same message in each girl's ear: "Come to the kitchen. We have to talk."

One at a time, the girls left the room. No one appeared to notice. Mrs. Porter had gone to the front desk to sit by the phone. A few guests were playing cards. No guests were leaving for their cottages. There was tacit agreement that everyone should stay together.

The kitchen was pitch-dark. The thunder and lightning seemed to be moving away, leaving only the steadily driving rain. And the wind. Maggie found the flashlight they kept by the door and switched it on.

"We have to find him!" were the first words out of Maggie's mouth.

"Exactly," Vicky said. "If I had to sit in there doing nothing for one minute more, I was going to go bananas. Storm or no storm, I want to search. He *must* be waiting somewhere for the storm to pass. Who would want to hurt Willy? And once he's found, your parents will change their minds. They can't sell the inn. They love it too much!"

Maggie had been thinking the same thoughts. It was her brother—and her inn, too. She wanted to get going. "There's foul-weather gear in the closet here. And extra flashlights."

Christie had been silent. The other two started in the direction of the closet. "Wait," she said, "There's something I have to tell you. I don't think it has anything to do with Willy's disappearance, but it might."

"What is it?" Vicky asked eagerly. "It's the woman with the red hair. Diane Griffith, right?"

"She's part of it." Christie started from the beginning—her discovery of the pool and meeting Mrs. Griffith.

"Why didn't you tell us?" Maggie couldn't believe Christie would keep this to herself.

"She said if I told anybody, I couldn't use it. I was a real jerk. I let my diving come before you guys. I'm really sorry."

"Forget about it. Just think—is there anything else? Anything that could be connected with Willy's disappearance?" Now that they'd decided to go outside, Maggie wanted to get moving, and although Christie's true confession was interesting, time was of the essence.

Sensing Maggie's mood, Christie abbreviated her tale. "People say she's crazy, a witch. You don't think she'd be so angry at me and everybody associated with the inn for stirring up the past that she'd do something to Willy?"

Here was a possible connection. Maggie had been pulling on a pair of fishermen's high rubber boots. Maybe Mrs. Griffith *was* unbalanced. Malvina had talked about the unhealthy attachment Mrs. Griffith had had to her daughter. Vicky's voice interrupted Maggie's wild thoughts.

"I don't believe it. She'd be more likely to go after *you*, Christie, but at least this gives us a starting point," Vicky said. She motioned Christie ahead. "Let's go. I believe you know the way."

Christie decided her own guilt could wait. She

knew when this was all over, she'd have to talk to her friends and figure out how she could have let herself get so sidetracked. The important thing now was to find Willy. Maggie scribbled a hasty note and left it on the counter with a small flashlight trained on it. Her parents couldn't miss it. She didn't want them to freak, thinking the girls had mysteriously disappeared, too.

Outside, the wind made all speech impossible. They started slowly down the wider path to the beach. It was the quickest way to Mrs. Griffith's. As they passed the thick woods surrounding the rear of the inn, they could see flickering lights. All Little Bittern had turned out to find Willy Porter.

The waves were crashing on the rocks they had so recently sat on, ignorant of the peril to come. The rain whipped across their faces, making it difficult to see, but they formed a chain with their hands and moved carefully across the shore until they came to the stairs up to the pool. Vicky slipped on a rock and came down hard, but she barely felt it, getting to her feet immediately. All thoughts were on Willy.

"We'll have to go on our hands and knees," Christie shouted. "Be careful not to fall backward. Reach up and hold on to the rail!"

It seemed hours before they were at the top, where, exhausted, they fell onto the sodden grass.

"Come on," Maggie screamed, and tried to run. The other two were close behind. They found the shorter flight of stairs, and at the last one, Maggie did dart forward.

Christie shone her flashlight and grabbed Maggie's

arm just in time. "The pool! It's right in front of you!" she cried.

The water was pitch-dark. They walked around it and set off for the house. The wind had abated slightly here in the meadow, but not the rain. They could see the house now, a dark shape looming up, a ghostly galleon. Not a single light showed, not even a candle.

Christie banged on the back door.

"She'll never hear you! Let me help you," Vicky cried. All three girls pounded against the wooden door, but no one came from inside to open it. Maggie turned the knob and pushed her shoulder against the heavy pine boards. The door didn't move. It was locked tight.

A hooded figure darted toward them from beneath the pines. Not until it was upon them did they see it. A scream froze in Christie's throat. She felt faint. They were all going to die. Willy had been killed and now it was their turn.

The wind blew the hood back. Hair tumbled forward—wet, silky auburn hair.

"Diane!" Christie pulled the woman toward her. "Where's your mother?"

"Vanished!" Diane Griffith's voice rose over the wind and the word sounded as desperate as the look on the woman's drenched face. "Vanished," she repeated, now in a tone of dull despair.

Reaching under the eaves for a key, Diane opened the back door, and the contrast was immediate. Away from the howling wind and pouring rain, Christie felt hopeful. They stood dripping by the doorway. Diane was the first to speak and the words came in a frantic rush, tumbling out into the room.

"I thought about what you said yesterday, Christie. You made it sound easy. I knew you were wrong about that. But I knew I had to come. I got here just before the storm broke. It's taken me all day to get my courage up. Or perhaps to lose my pride," she added ruefully.

"No one was in the house, but Mother always let the servants go to the mainland for holidays, and I had a feeling I knew where she'd be, although I was worried with the storm approaching."

"Where was that?" Vicky asked curiously. Diane was speaking more calmly now.

"On the shore, just below the house. It's her favorite walk, and there's a place to sit there, a small deck, roofed over. The beach peas climb up the sides. I played there as a child. And I was right—she was there."

Christie took a deep breath.

"At first, she didn't move; then she began to cry. I ran to her, and we held each other hard. All our words seemed to come at once. Years of words." The words were flowing quickly from Diane Griffith's lips again.

"We started up the stairs. The storm was near. I remembered I'd left the bag I was carrying down at the beach. I didn't want the tide to take it. She laughed and told me to go back, said we had all the time in the world." Diane's voice caught. "Then she called from the top, quite agitated: 'Something's wrong! I have to go! It mustn't wait. Something evil.' I screamed at her to wait for me, but by the time I got there, she was gone. Vanished into thin air. Not in the house, the woods, the meadow. I've been searching ever since."

"My brother—he's only ten—is missing, too. *Please,* Miss Griffith, can you think what your mother might have meant?" Maggie begged.

"No, it doesn't make any sense. Everything was fine; then it was almost as if she had seen a ghost. My mother believes she can sometimes see and hear things other people can't. I used to think it was nonsense. I'm not sure I do anymore. I don't know whether Christie has told you my story, but Mother begged me not to go. She said she saw tragedy and death. I didn't listen."

"We have to keep looking! Is the phone still out?" Christie had one hand on the door. She wished Maggie hadn't heard the word *death.* But of course she had. Her face looked like a chalkboard where someone had erased every word except *fear.*

Diane lifted the receiver. "Yes. And the electricity, too."

There was only the sound of the storm, no comforting hum from the refrigerator. The storm swirled violently around the house, rattling the windows and cracking branches.

"Let's go," Christie instructed briskly. "Two and two. We'll meet back here every thirty minutes. You can leave the door unlocked, can't you?"

Diane Griffith nodded. "Marie must have locked it

on her way out. It's usually open. Mother uses the front door to go to the beach, and I came in that way."

"Maggie," Christie continued, "you and Vicky go in the direction of the inn; we'll go this way."

They went out into the teeming darkness again and started to search. The wind howled. It seemed louder after their time indoors. Maggie wanted to cover her ears, or scream to try to drown out the noise.

Vicky was at one end of the meadow. Maggie made her way to the pool. Next to the pool stood a small windowless shed. The padlock on the door hung open. It was slippery in her fingers and she dropped it on the concrete, pulling at the door. The wind made it almost impossible to open.

Inside, a flashlight lit the tiny space. Caroline Griffith was sitting next to Willy, who was stretched out on the floor, his eyes closed. She was holding his hand. She put a finger to her lips. Her long white hair had escaped from its pins and hung down below her shoulders in disarray. The flashlight beam cast strange shadows on her face. Maggie gasped. The old woman was a witch!

"He may be slightly concussed—I didn't want to move him. Although he is conscious. He knows I'm here, but he doesn't know what happened or how he got in the shed. My—my daughter is probably in the house. I couldn't open the door against the wind to get her. Tell her to go to the inn at once. Your parents must be worried sick!" The old woman's compassionate tone quickly dispelled Maggie's first impression and she burst into tears.

Her brother was alive! Alive and all right. "Willy, it's Mags. Everything's going to be fine!" His eyes fluttered open.

"Now, don't waste time blubbering. Plenty of time for that later. We've got to get him a doctor."

"And," Caroline Griffith continued grimly, "we've got to find out who did this."

❖Chapter Ten

MAGGIE RAN TO THE END OF THE MEADOW, where she could just make out something moving. She hoped it was Vicky, and it was.

"He's safe! He's with Mrs. Griffith in the shed over there. I'm going to the inn for help. You go back and tell the others. It's been almost thirty minutes, so they'll be at the house soon."

"Maggie, you can't go alone! Wait and we'll go together."

Maggie was adamant. "There isn't time. We don't know where Christie and Diane are looking. I have to go *now!* He needs a doctor, and whoever did this could be escaping! I'll be careful."

Vicky tried to hold on to her friend, but Maggie pulled away and set out for home. She knew she could make better time through the woods. If she just kept going in the general direction, she was bound to link up with one of the inn's paths.

As she pushed branches from her face, she felt relief—and anger. What kind of monster would do such a thing to a child! Willy had obviously been knocked out and put into the shed. It could have been a day or days before anyone thought to look for him there.

But how did Mrs. Griffith know? Maggie remembered Diane's description—that Caroline Griffith had appeared to see something, something evil. Was she clairvoyant? Was the whole island under a spell! Maggie ran forward. She tripped over a root that her flashlight hadn't picked up. To save herself from falling, she grabbed at the nearest tree, a pine, and felt the skin on her hand tearing.

She stopped, aware of the pain and fearful that she had gotten lost. She couldn't do anything right! She should have listened to Vicky. Now she would delay things and end up having people looking for *her*. She started to sob; then a familiar shape to the right caught in the beam of light. It was their rock, the one she and Charlene had discovered Maggie's first summer on the island. She could find her way to the inn from here blindfolded, which was just about what she was. She patted the rough granite as she sped by. It was like an old friend.

Ten minutes later, she ran up the front steps and into the lobby, where her mother was keeping a vigil by the phone.

"Mom! Oh, Mom! He's alive and okay. Well, almost okay. He needs a doctor, because Mrs. Griffith thinks he may be concussed, but . . ."

For an instant Julia Porter stood still, her daughter's words reaching her ears but not her consciousness; then the realization that her son was all right burst upon her and she rushed, sobbing, to hold Maggie tightly.

"Thank God! Where is he? How did you find him?"

The guests heard the commotion and, fearing the worst, hung back in the doorway. Maggie turned to them, her eyes sparkling. "It's all right! He's going to be fine! We found him!"

Everything happened very quickly after that. Someone had the presence of mind to go outside and ring the large bell suspended from a mast next to the flagpole. The rescue workers, including Ned Porter and the Sanfords, arrived rapidly. Darnell set off for the doctor. Another Sanford got on the CB in his truck to notify the state police and the Coast Guard. Then the rest of Christie & Company arrived with Diane Griffith. They'd come by way of the beach, since Marie and her husband had taken Mrs. Griffith's car to the ferry.

"Maggie! We knew you'd get here!" Christie yelled when she saw her friend. She and Vicky exchanged glances of great relief. Neither had wanted to give voice to the fears they had for their friend's safety as she made her way through the dark woods with a madman loose.

A madman—or madwoman. Who? That was the question on everyone's minds.

The Porters jumped in another car and set off for the Griffith house, followed by most of the island in whatever vehicles were at hand.

When Mrs. Griffith saw them all crowding in the tiny doorway of her shed, she allowed herself a small smile. "Nice to see you. Why don't we go on up to the house and my daughter will make us some coffee. I think this child needs to be with his mother and father."

It became obvious no one would sleep much that night. The doctor had declared Willy fit to be moved. "Good thing he has such a hard head," he'd said. And now that the storm was almost over, the Coast Guard had airlifted him off the island in a helicopter, with Julia Porter by his side. Maggie was glad Willy was conscious enough to enjoy the adventure. Before he left, he'd turned to her, whispering, "Sammy Compton is going to be so jealous!" and she'd known he was on the mend. Mrs. Porter was happy to be getting her son off the island. Before she climbed into the helicopter, she told her husband she thought they should send Willy to his grandparents for the rest of the summer—and maybe Maggie, too.

Maggie was stunned. She had thought that once they found Willy, everything would be all right, but of course it wasn't. Her parents still intended to sell the Blue Heron, and her life on Little Bittern would be gone forever.

Christie & Company plus George returned to the inn with Mr. Porter, a dejected group. They hadn't joined the others drinking coffee at Mrs. Griffith's, although Christie felt a glimmer of pride when she saw Diane take her mother's arm and the two exchange a loving glance. It also made her feel hopeful. If that could turn out happily ever after, why not everything else?

Guests not lodged in the main part of the inn had bedded down as best they could in the living room.

136

The electricity and phone were still out, but they now had the loan of a truck with a CB. They weren't cut off from the world, even though it felt like that as the long night dragged on.

The girls did not even pretend to sleep; they sat in the kitchen with George.

"How can we possibly solve this if Willy can't remember what happened to him?" Vicky asked. "And Mrs. Griffith said she has no idea how he could have ended up in her pool shed."

"The padlock isn't kept closed. I noticed that the first time I went there to swim," Christie said. "Anyone snooping around there would know. It was probably closed after Willy was left inside, but Mrs. Griffith would have been able to open it. I'm beginning to think she's pretty amazing."

"Let's start asking questions—and make a list. We're forgetting all our detective skills," Maggie said. There was a frenetic undercurrent to her words. Morning would bring a general exodus from the inn. The ferry to the mainland would be packed. They had to solve this before then!

"You last saw Willy at four o'clock, right, George?" Christie began taking notes on the back of a paper place mat.

"Right," George said, "and it takes Willy about half an hour to ride home from Green Harbor, more if he sees something interesting along the way."

"So let's say Willy got here just before five. Everybody was down at the beach for cocktails. Everybody except the person who attacked him and hid the bike."

"The police will be able to check the bike for fingerprints, but I'll bet whoever did it wore gloves," Maggie said.

They made a list of everyone on the beach and tried to think of a motive.

"It has to be tied in to all the other things happening!" Vicky exclaimed. "We need to find the link."

George spoke, slowly, as usual, and his deep voice added emphasis to his words. "Seems like all the things are things intended to shut a place like this down. When they didn't work, the person got desperate."

"And it worked," Maggie said glumly.

Dawn was beginning to streak across the sky. The only traces of the storm were the branches littering the ground and the debris, natural and man-made, washed up on the beach. The air was clear and fresh.

It was going to be a perfect Maine day.

George had gone home and the girls had fallen asleep slumped over the kitchen table. The inn was completely quiet. Maggie sat up. She was stiff and sore. The cut on her hand hurt. She stood up. The first ferry was at six. No one would have been able to get off the island last night in the storm. This was their last chance. She checked the phone and electricity—still out—then gently shook the others awake.

"We have to keep watch," she said. "See who leaves first, who's in a hurry."

The girls tiptoed out the back door and scattered to various locations to keep a lookout. Christie took the front door, Vicky the back, Maggie the cabins. Nothing stirred.

Maggie yawned. The birds were beginning to wake. They filled the early-morning air with their cries. Something else filled the air—the steady *tap, tap, tap* of typing. Paul Corcoran? Up at dawn with an inspiration? She crept down the path to the cabin he'd been using and looked in the window.

She gasped. No one was there!

Carefully, she opened the door, and the mystery was solved. A squirrel leapt from the desk and proceeded to scold Maggie for interrupting him. A squirrel that could touch-type? Maggie started to laugh, then realized what the squirrel had done. It had pressed a button, not a typewriter key. A button on a small cassette player. Now why would Paul want people to think he was working when he wasn't? DO NOT DISTURB. WRITER AT WORK. What an alibi! She opened the closet and the last pieces of the puzzle magically fell into place. Leaning against the back was Darnell's hunting rifle. Willy's mask was hanging from a hook, along with the jacket he'd had on at the Fish Fry. Maggie didn't need to see any more. She grabbed the cassette player and turned for the door.

Paul Corcoran was there watching her, an ugly twisted smile on his lips. She screamed and threw the player with all her might directly at his face. He was too quick for her and slammed the door, pausing to turn the key in the lock before running down the path. Maggie didn't waste any time. Stopping only to pick up the tape, she pushed open a window, climbed out, and ran after him.

"Stop him!" she shouted as loudly as she could. "Stop Paul!" She didn't know who would hear her, yet she was counting on Christie & Company. She kept yelling for help as she got closer to the inn, but Paul Corcoran had gotten a head start. He was climbing into the truck—the one with the CB—just as Vicky and Christie came around the corner in response to her cries.

"Bikes! We've got to get to the Sanfords' radio and keep him from getting on the boat."

The three girls grabbed their bikes and set off down the drive as fast as they could. There was no time to tell Mr. Porter. Vicky and Christie had no idea what was going on, but they trusted Maggie. She told them what she'd discovered as they pedaled furiously. "Paul Corcoran! That wimp!" Christie said, nearly toppling over.

Waking George and Darnell, they called the state police first, then began alerting the island.

"Come on. Get in the car! We've got to get your Dad. And, by gorry, this is one I don't want to miss." Darnell was as excited as a kid.

Nobody else within range of a CB or roused by a neighbor wanted to miss it, either. After the police, the first person they had called was Charlene, who quickly marshaled every kid and every bike on the island. When Paul Corcoran came screeching into the landing just before the *Miss Hattie* pulled out for her six o'clock crossing, the pickup was barricaded by several solid rows of bikes, quickly augmented by adults who simply stood quietly with their arms folded across their chests.

He gave one feeble try. "What's going on here? Has this place gone crazy? Let me on the boat!"

"You're not going anywhere, mister." Darnell had waited a lifetime to say something like that. The crowd moved in closer. Several of the little kids blew their bike horns.

"You just stay put," Darnell added.

Paul Corcoran rolled up the window, then a moment later rolled it down. "It wasn't all me, anyway," he spat out at Maggie venomously. "Go ask your Aunt Lucinda and Uncle Bob how much they paid me to close down the Blue Heron Inn!"

Willy and Julia Porter were home. Even though he felt great, Willy was enjoying the special attention his hospitalization was bringing him. He was wrapped in a blanket, reclining on one of the sofas in the Blue Heron's living room. An enormous dish of warm blueberry cobbler with vanilla ice cream sat on the coffee table in front of him.

"I still can't believe it," Julia Porter said. "We trusted them. They were our friends. How could they do such a thing?"

Her husband answered, tight-lipped. "Greed, pure and simple. Sure, I knew Bob was a pretty materialistic guy and some of his values were not the same as ours, but I never thought he'd pay someone to drive me out of business just so he could set up his daughter and son-in-law in such a ridiculous scheme."

Maggie was having a hard time keeping her mouth shut. She desperately wanted someone to say she had been right about the Bishops all along. George and Darnell Sanford were at Willy's welcome-home party and it was George who granted Maggie's unspoken wish.

"You never liked them, did you, Mags? Never trusted them."

Mr. Porter looked at his daughter sheepishly. "I should have listened to you. Maybe I'm *not* cut out to be a businessman."

The first words were what Maggie had longed to hear, but not the last. Before she could say anything, Vicky spoke up.

"My parents are businesspeople. They trust people all the time, and they would never resort to the tactics the Bishops used. Although I guess Mr. and Mrs. Bishop didn't know how far Paul Corcoran was going. They were at Hap Hotchkiss's house and never knew Willy was missing, remember, or that the tires had been shot."

"It's something, but not much. They were at his house, missing our lobster, to cook up a deal with him to run the inn as part of a chain of resort hotels," Maggie said vehemently.

"Pretty comical in one way." Darnell laughed. "Can you imagine those two addle-brained St. Clairs running anything anywhere except into the ground!"

Julia looked at her son. "It's time for you to go to bed. Remember, the doctor said you shouldn't get overtired."

"Oh, Ma," Willy complained. "I miss out on everything."

Mrs. Porter looked at her husband. She wished

Willy had been anywhere except the inn when Paul Corcoran was looking for a target. He'd hit the boy hard enough to knock him out. If it hadn't been for Caroline Griffith . . . and Maggie and her friends, too. She went over and kissed her daughter on the top of her curly head. She'd been doing things like that a lot lately. Maggie beamed.

"Bed," Julia said firmly, and helped Willy get up.

"We have to get going, too," Darnell said. "Thanks for dessert."

Christie & Company piled up the dishes and took them into the kitchen. They were heading down to their cottage, but they had no intention of going to sleep. Finally, all the pieces had fallen into place when the Porters received a call from the state police late in the afternoon, detailing Paul Corcoran's confession and implication of the Bishops. Apparently, their plans weren't known by the St. Clairs, whose reaction had been one of total repulsion. "Run that decrepit old inn! Duh! I'd rather die first!" Bobbie had reportedly objected. Her husband had also been stunned. "Work there! There's nobody on that island!" The girls weren't sure whether it was the idea of work or the lack of people that turned him off the most.

Back at the cabin, they quickly got ready for bed and sat on the old couch in front of the bay window. It was dark out, but the stars were shining brightly and the moon, almost half-full, had risen.

"It's pathetic, really. He needed the money to keep writing. He told the police he's close to finishing the Great American Novel. His aunt flatly refused to give him any more funds and he got mad, decided he'd show *her*. But he needed more time. Somehow, the Bishops found this out. He probably opened his heart to Lucinda over 'drinkies' one night." Vicky's voice was scornful.

"I saw him on the path the first morning you were here, almost bumped into him. He must have put the dead mouse in his aunt's bag then. And changed the paprika tins," Maggie added. "But I put him out of my mind. He was . . . well, so drab."

"Exactly," Christie said, picking up the thread. "Although he probably got a real charge out of seeing his aunt get all upset. And the snake in that woman's bed would have caused a scene, too, if Malvina hadn't found it."

"And the dead seagull, don't forget."

"I think little Paul likes to scare people. Makes him feel powerful," Maggie suggested. "The *Friday the Thirteenth* mask, everything. I wonder what his book is about? Sounds like he started to live it."

"Yeah, but the business with Willy and taking Darnell's gun—that was way beyond a Halloween mask," Christie said soberly. "He picked on a child, someone weaker. He didn't dare attack an adult."

"And now," Maggie said cheerfully, "he's going away for a long, long time—kidnapping, assault, whole bunches of things. He'll have lots of time to write in prison."

"What about the Bishops and Hap? What will happen to them?" Vicky asked.

"Hap swears he didn't know anything about the plot to close down the inn, and he may be telling the truth. The Bishops wouldn't have wanted too many people to know, but I have my doubts. He was trying to buy Sanford Cove. Can't you just see it as a quaint marina to go with whatever they were going to put here? Anyway, at the moment, *Uncle* Bob and *Aunt* Lucinda have hired a very expensive lawyer and they'll try to pin everything on Paul, but they did write him several checks to play those dirty tricks, checks he cashed. In some perverted way, they think anything to help their precious Bobbie is justified."

"Your poor parents, Mags. They're so trusting. This is going to change all that," Christie said.

"My parents! Never. Wait awhile. Their heads will be back in the stratosphere, especially Dad's. They're not selling the inn, you know. Mom's getting a little feisty. 'I'm certainly not going to give them the satisfaction of closing now!' I heard her tell Dad. Besides, Sybil Corcoran is so mortified over Paul that she's writing an article giving the Blue Heron a trillion stars—which it deserves."

The girls laughed. Vicky yawned. "Was it just last Saturday we were at the dance? What a week!"

Acknowledging the understatement, the girls went to bed.

❖ Epilogue

A CHORUS OF OOHS AND AAHS ROSE FROM the crowd gathered on the hill overlooking the harbor. The first firework had started as a tiny golden pinprick of light, then exploded into a chrysanthemum, dropping petals of gold into the dark water. Maggie was lying on her back, her friends were next to her, and George sat by her side. Mrs. Griffith and Diane were sitting behind them.

"Boom!" the noise reverberated across the island. Christie heard Caroline Griffith laugh in delight.

As soon as the phones were working, Mrs. Griffith had called to find out how Willy was. She had never offered an explanation for how she knew where he was, and Christie knew none would ever come. Mrs. Griffith had also asked to speak to Christie. She told her she wanted her to use the pool—bringing her friends—and to come see them at the house. Diane was staying for the summer and then their plans weren't clear. Caroline might go to New York with her daughter. Diane might stay longer.

A series of brightly colored rockets shot rapidly into the night sky and streamed back down in a cascade of emerald, scarlet, and silver.

Vicky sat up. "I know who she is!" She hadn't realized she'd spoken so loudly. Maggie and Christie sat up, too, "Who?" Maggie asked. Vicky lowered her voice. "Diane Griffith. That's not her name. I mean it is her name, except it's not her stage name. That's Persephone Hamilton. She was a sensation on Broadway for years, then dropped out of sight. But I bet she's doing voice-overs now. I know I've heard her!"

The sky was filled with fireworks, the crowd growing more ecstatic with each new burst, but Maggie was lost in thought.

"And there shall be no spring, no warmth, no harvest on the earth until my daughter, Persephone, returns to me," the goddess Demeter told Zeus. "Hades, Lord of the Underworld, must release her."

Demeter kept her word and the earth was plunged into bitter cold. The fruits turned to ice on the trees and the ground froze as solid as the grieving mother's heart. The maiden also mourned and regretted the temptation that had caused her to stray from her mother's meadow. Finally, Zeus commanded her return, and the joy of the reunion caused the plants to flower once more. The air was warm and fragrant. But Persephone had eaten one red pomegranate seed, offered by Hades, and was bound to return for a portion of each year. Then it would be winter until the next reunion.

Maggie turned and looked at the mother and daughter behind her: the mother and daughter of joyous summer.

Mothers and daughters, all so alike, so different. It was hard to figure it out. She shook her head.

Then she felt George's hand cover hers. "It all came out right, Maggie. You did it. That Christie and Company of yours. You should be proud."

And she was.